**Praise for *USA TODAY* bestselling author
Kimberly Raye**

"Kimberly Raye's *A Body to Die For* is fun and
sexy, filled with sensual details, secrets and
heartwarming characters—as well as humor
in the most unexpected places."
—*RT Book Reviews*

"*Dead Sexy* by Kimberly Raye
is funny and exciting—with great sex,
characters and plot twists."
—*RT Book Reviews*

"Kimberly Raye has done a wonderful job of
creating characters that are unique
and imaginative!"
—*Romance Reviews Today* on *Dead and Dateless*

"A laugh-out-loud, sexy, heartwarming story
and a wonderful heroine."
—*RT Book Reviews* on *Drop Dead Gorgeous*

Dear Reader,

It's always hot in Texas, but it's blazing-hot this month thanks to Cole Chisholm, the last of the notorious Chisholm brothers and the star of my newest novel, *Texas Outlaws: Cole*. Cole is a professional bronc rider and the sexiest bachelor on the professional rodeo circuit. He's also the hottest commodity among the single women of Lost Gun, Texas, and so the race is on to see who can lasso him to the altar first.

The lucky winner? Resident bad girl Nikki Barbie. Nikki comes from a long line of wild and wicked women—particularly a mother who thinks men are only good for one thing. The thing is, Nikki isn't half as wild in the bedroom as she is in the kitchen. She wants to become a professional chef and she's this close to making her dream come true. But when her sisters get married and she becomes her mother's last great hope to continue the family's risqué reputation, Nikki knows she has to get the woman off her back once and for all. The only way to do that? Tie the knot.

When Nikki makes her proposition—a marriage of convenience followed by a quickie divorce—Cole agrees. It's the perfect setup. That is, until things start to get complicated thanks to a lot of money from an old bank heist, an unexpected robbery and a bad case of lust.

Sit back, relax and enjoy as Cole and Nikki do their best to recover the money, clear Cole's good name and not fall in love!

Much love from deep in the heart,

Kimberly Raye

P.S. Don't forget to stop by and visit me on the web at www.kimberlyraye.com or friend me on Facebook. I love hearing from readers!

Texas Outlaws: Cole

—

Kimberly Raye

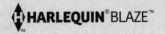

ISBN-13: 978-0-373-79792-9

TEXAS OUTLAWS: COLE

Copyright © 2014 by Kimberly Groff

Printed in U.S.A.

H HARLEQUIN®
TM www.Harlequin.com

ABOUT THE AUTHOR

USA TODAY bestselling author Kimberly Raye started her first novel in high school and has been writing ever since. To date, she's published more than fifty novels, two of them prestigious RITA® Award nominees. She's also been nominated by *RT Book Reviews* for several Reviewer's Choice Awards, as well as a career achievement award. Currently she is writing a romantic vampire mystery series for Ballantine Books that is in development with ABC for a television pilot. She also writes steamy contemporary reads for Harlequin's Blaze line. Kim lives deep in the heart of the Texas Hill Country with her very own cowboy, Curt, and their young children. She's an avid reader who loves Diet Dr Pepper, chocolate, Toby Keith, chocolate, alpha males (*especially* vampires) and chocolate. Kim also loves to hear from readers. You can visit her online at www.kimberlyraye.com.

Books by Kimberly Raye

For Debbie Villanueva Dimas,

My long-time BFF
and the best godmother in the entire world!

You're the best and we love you!

Prologue

"HERE'S THE LAST of it." Cole Unger Chisholm stood in the four-foot-deep hole and pulled the small metal coffee can from the freshly turned dirt before handing it to his brother.

"We don't know that for sure." Jesse Chisholm was the oldest Chisholm and the only reason Cole had spent nearly every night for the past three months digging up a storm. When he wasn't busting his ass on the pro rodeo circuit, that is.

At twenty-eight, Cole was pro rodeo's reigning saddle-bronc star with a record-setting five championships under his belt. He was also the favorite to take home a sixth in just a few short weeks in Vegas.

If he could finish up with this mess and get back to his normal practice schedule. As it was, he'd been spending every free moment in his hometown of Lost Gun, Texas, helping his two brothers dig up an entire fifty-acre pasture to find the money that their criminal father had stolen from a local bank over fifteen years ago. *Before* the old man had set himself on fire and gone up in a blaze of glory.

They'd hit the mother lode approximately three months ago when Billy had unearthed a small metal box. They'd all been convinced they'd found the missing one hundred thousand dollars, until they'd counted the contents to find only a measly one thousand. Since then, they'd unearthed ninety-eight more containers—everything from a metal lock box, to rusted-out coffee cans, to a dozen shoe boxes—each containing exactly one grand.

"This is the hundredth container," Cole said, taking a swig from a water bottle. "This has to be it."

"Most likely," Jesse agreed, but he wasn't placing any bets, not until he went through the contents.

"Just count it so we can get out of here." Cole took another swig before chucking the bottle to a nearby trash pile. "I'd like to get out of here sometime before my next rodeo."

"Tired, big brother?" Billy, Cole's youngest brother, gave him a knowing glance. "Or are you just anxious to get back home so you can lick your wounds since Jake and Jimmy beat you to the punch and took the Barbie sisters off the market?"

"There's still one left." Not that Cole had his sights set on sister number three. Nicole Barbie had been just a kid when they were growing up, a good six years younger than Cole, and so he'd never paid her no nevermind. Rather, he'd been fixated on her two older sisters. He'd dated them both off and on over the years. Nothing serious, but then the Barbie sisters didn't do serious. They were the baddest bad girls in town.

Once upon a time, that is.

Until last month when his best buds Jimmy and Jake Barber had popped the question and the girls had actually said yes.

Cole still couldn't believe it. Out of all the women he knew, Crystal and April didn't seem like the marrying type.

And Cole Chisholm knew the marrying kind. Since both of his brothers had recently settled down, Cole was now the only single Chisholm left. He'd had a slew of women after him over the past few months, particularly since he'd been spending so much time hanging around Lost Gun, helping Billy and Jesse dig up the money.

Susie Carlisle had baked him three dozen brownies and Jenny Farmer had brought him fresh canned preserves. Delilah Martin had even made her prize-winning meatloaf. And while Cole had nothing against a good hunk of meat, he was smart enough to know that enjoying even one bite would send the wrong message—namely that he was ready to slow down and settle down.

Like hell.

"Well? How much is there?" he asked Jesse.

"Yeah," Billy chimed in. He was the youngest Chisholm, and just as anxious to be done with the digging as Cole. Albeit for different reasons. Like Jesse who'd found the love of his life, Billy had recently traded in his bachelor status to play house with his one and only. Both men were set to tie the knot after the finals in Vegas. "What's the verdict?"

"Hold your horses." Jesse peeled off bills one after the other. "I'm counting."

Cole leaned on the edge of the shovel and stared over the top of the hole at the pastureland surrounding them. It was just a few minutes shy of sunrise and a faint orange glow lit the horizon. They usually started digging late at night, under the cover of darkness, but it was Saturday. *The* Saturday, and so Jesse had said to hell with caution.

Cole eyed the rutted ground. They'd tried to fill in the holes so as not to raise any red flags. The people of Lost Gun, along with a mess of fortune hunters, had been looking for Silas Chisholm's missing fortune for years now. If word got out that his three sons had actually found the money, the place would be crawling with people.

But Cole, Jesse and Billy intended to be the only ones to dig up their father's past. Once they had every penny present and accounted for, they intended to give it back to the town and kill the rumors that had been circulating about them once and for all.

That they'd been in on it. That they'd secretly been spending the cash over the years. That they were every bit as worthless as their father.

They hadn't even known about the money until a few months ago when Jesse had uncovered a connection between Silas and the town's most notorious moonshiner. Unfortunately, Big Earl Jessup wasn't the man he used to be. In his nineties now, his old-timer's had set in. He could no longer whip up his infamous White Lightning moonshine any more than he could remember where he'd buried the money from the bank heist committed by his good friend and partner in crime, Silas Chisholm.

The plan had been for Silas to hand off the money to Big Earl, who would then bury it until the fuss died down. Then they would both dig it back up at a later time and enjoy the spoils. But then Silas had set himself on fire and drawn a wave of media attention to their small Texas town. The story had attracted tons of reporters and earned a spot on a Discovery Channel documentary called *Famous Texas Outlaws*. Most recently, a "Where Are They Now?" episode had aired on the documentary's tenth anniversary.

Bottom line, Big Earl had sat on the money for so long that he'd eventually forgotten where he'd buried it all. And so Cole and his brothers, along with Big

Earl's great granddaughter, Casey, had been digging up the old man's pasture for the past three months.

"This is it," Jesse announced, stashing the rolls of cash back inside the coffee can. "One hundred thousand dollars."

"Finally," Cole muttered.

While he was glad they'd recovered the money and he wanted to see the Chisholm name cleared, he wasn't as haunted by it as his oldest brother. No, he'd killed himself shoveling dirt for Jesse. So that his oldest brother could make peace with the past.

Cole wasn't half as anxious to make peace as he was just to forget. To leave the memories where they belonged—way, *way* behind him—and focus on the future. His RV was packed and waiting back at the prime stretch of land he'd purchased on the outskirts of town. The perfect spot to breed some prime, Grade A horseflesh if he ever got the notion.

A slim possibility because Cole liked moving around, traveling, *living*.

He'd spent his entire childhood barely existing. Food had been in short supply. Money had been practically nonexistent. And love? He'd had his brothers, but Silas had been a piss-poor excuse for a father. There'd been too much misery, too many days spent feeling like he was being suffocated by his situation, snuffed out, beaten down. He'd been so close to giving up.

But then legendary bull rider Pete Gunner had taken him and his brothers in and helped them become rodeo's best and most notorious. Cole was now one of the infamous Lost Boys—*the* hottest group of riders on the circuit, so named because they all hailed from the same small town.

For him, it was all about living life now rather than merely enduring it. About feeling the rush of adrenaline when he climbed onto the back of a bronc, smelling the fresh dirt that kicked up around him, hearing the thunder of his own heart, seeing the whites of his knuckles as he held tight to the reins and gave the ride everything he had.

He felt alive then. *Free.*

All the more reason to get back out on the road.

"Move your ass." Billy reached out a hand to Cole and helped him out of the hole. "We've got an hour to get back to town and get cleaned up before we head over to the church. Jimmy and Jake will kill us if we're late."

Yep, he was leaving, all right.

After he stuffed himself into a tuxedo and walked some blushing bridesmaid down the aisle.

"I'll put in a call to the sheriff and see if I can set up a meeting for tomorrow morning so we can get this money back to its rightful owner." Jesse started gathering up their tools. "In the meantime, we've got a wedding to get to."

1

IT WAS THE SECOND biggest wedding the small town of Lost Gun, Texas, had ever seen. Next in line only to the marriage of pro bull-riding legend Pete Gunner who'd married his one and only earlier that year.

Nikki Barbie hadn't been in attendance at that particular event because she'd been home nursing a bad case of strep.

Thankfully.

Weddings were definitely not her thing.

The truth struck as she stood to the right of the minister of the Lost Gun First Baptist Church and listened to her two oldest sisters vow to "love, honor and cherish."

Crystal and April were marrying the Barber twins in a massive double-wedding ceremony, complete with a fairy-tale theme that translated in the form of castle-shaped sugar-cookie favors and a live butterfly release. Jimmy and Jake Barber were the hottest team ropers on the rodeo circuit and members of the Lost Boys, which meant that in addition to the few hundred guests, there were at least a dozen reporters crowded inside the sanctuary. Snapping pictures. Documenting memories.

This was definitely the worst day of her life.

And not just because she was wearing a floor-length, pink satin dress, complete with parasol *and* matching sandals.

Raylene Barbie—Nikki's mother and owner of The Giddyup, Lost Gun's oldest and most popular honky-tonk—was the culprit behind the tragic state of Nikki's life. Raylene was a card-carrying, ball-busting Southern bad girl who would sooner guzzle a lukewarm beer than narrow down her options and give up her freedom to just one man.

Not that she didn't like men. Quite the opposite. She appreciated a good hunk of beefcake as much as the next red-blooded woman. More so, in fact. Raylene Barbie went through men faster than the members of the ladies' auxiliary went through panty hose.

Men were good for one thing, and it had nothing to do with any sort of happily ever after. They were fun. Exciting. And very, very temporary.

Which explained why she sat in the front row and stared at her youngest daughter as if she were the last beer in the cooler at a Fourth of July picnic.

Nikki was so screwed.

She swallowed the bile that rose in her throat and tried to focus on the positive. At least her mother had shown up for the wedding, which had made Crystal and April two happy campers. The woman had been giving them both the silent treatment since they'd announced their engagement six weeks ago, and so there had been speculation about her putting in an appearance on *the* most important day in their lives. But she'd come through, even if only out of desperate hope that they would both back out at the last minute.

Nikki drew a much-needed breath and tried to settle the gymnastics routine currently going on in her stomach. Sweat beaded on her upper lip. Her hands went damp and she had to readjust her grip on the heavy bridesmaid's bouquet.

Tulips, of all things. And baby's breath. And while the entire thing looked sweet and delicate, that was the point entirely. The Barbie sisters didn't *do* sweet and delicate. Crystal and April lived in hot-pink cowboy boots, itty-bitty tank tops and black leather miniskirts. They were bold. Beautiful. *Bad.*

Once upon a time.

They'd traded in their racy clothing for two of the biggest, most poofiest white dresses this side of the Rio Grande. They were giving up their old ways. Getting married. Settling down.

Nikki sucked in a much-needed breath. Geez, it was hot. And stuffy. And bright.

Daytime weddings should be outlawed. Particularly when they took place at a church where the reverend prided himself on locking in the temperature at an economy-saving seventy-five degrees.

Sunlight streamed through the stained-glass windows of the sanctuary, temporarily blinding her. She blinked and swallowed against a rising wave of nausea and the crazy urge to call a halt to the entire ceremony.

I object!

If Crystal and April weren't sane enough to do it themselves, then she needed to step up. To preserve her own sanity.

Her lips parted. Her tongue moved. Her voice box squeaked—

The sound of a throat clearing cut her off before she could blurt out the first word. Her gaze snapped up and collided with the best man who stood directly across from her.

Cole Unger Chisholm, pro rodeo's biggest and best saddle-bronc rider, narrowed his gaze as if to say "Stay out of it," and her own gaze narrowed.

She clamped her lips shut and frowned. He had a lot of nerve. He was the crazy one. The impulsive wild card who prided himself on doing the outlandish. From standing upright on a bucking bronc during the last few seconds of his ride, to flipping off reporters when they got a little too close, Cole was the quintessential bad boy. The last one left now that the rest of the infamous Lost Boys were officially off the market.

He was the one more likely to make a scene and blow the ceremony. He was outlandish. Unpredictable.

And damned good-looking.

He wore a black tuxedo jacket that outlined his broad shoulders. A crisp white shirt, starched Wranglers and spit-polished black cowboy boots completed the outfit. His usually long and unkempt brown hair had been pulled back to tone down the bad boy look, but the shadow covering his jaw killed the effort. He still looked like every woman's wet dream. The perfect man for a one-night stand.

If Nikki had been into one-night stands.

She wasn't, even if she had entertained a few choice fantasies about Mr. Saddle-bronc champion. But those were her own most private thoughts. It wasn't as if she meant to act on them. *Ever.* Which was the main reason she was about to freak fifty ways to Sunday.

Despite her own reputation as a bona fide bad girl, she wasn't the real deal like her two older sisters. She hated late nights and loud music and too much booze. Three very important truths she'd managed to hide from her mother up to this point because Raylene's attention had always been fixated on the older girls. They'd been her pride and joy. Two chips off the old block.

Until now.

"...marriage is a joyous union between two souls that marks the beginning of a new life together..." the minister went on, and reality weighed down on Nikki.

Crystal, her oldest sister and the one everyone had expected to follow in Raylene's footsteps and take over the honky-tonk, was getting *married,* of all things. Ditto for April. They'd both given up their wild and wicked ways, and their jobs as head bartender and chief bar maid, to pledge their undying devotion. Even more, they were packing up and moving to a ranch over an hour away, and Nikki would be the only one left to help Raylene.

No more hiding out in the kitchen, plotting her culinary future while she whipped up the typical bar food—everything from chicken wings to nachos. No more studying her butt off in the back room while her mom and sisters kept the party going out front. No more applying for sous-chef positions with a handful of Houston's top restaurants.

She was the only daughter left now. Her mother's last hope.

She swallowed again and tried to ignore the churning in the pit of her stomach. A drop of sweat tickled its way down Nikki's right temple. The razor burn on her legs prickled.

"…take this man to be your lawfully wedded husband…"

She blew out a deep breath and inhaled again. Her nostrils burned with the sickeningly sweet scent of flowers coupled with the half gallon of sickly sweet *eau de gag me* Margie Waltrip, Lost Gun's one and only wedding coordinator, had sprayed her with prior to the walk down the church aisle. Her stomach pitched and rolled.

"…and do you take this woman to be your lawfully wedded wife…"

Easy. Just breathe. In. Out. In. Out.

"…by the power vested in me, I pronounce each of you man and wife. Husbands, you may kiss your brides!"

She was not going to throw up, despite the blinding light and the overwhelming smell and her mother's hopeful stare.

Rather, she was going to paste a smile on her face and waltz back up the aisle with the rest of the wedding party.

Or waddle, which was about all she could manage in the huge dress.

And then she was going to find her way out of the

maze of tulle and flowers, hunt down the church's nearest exit and run for her life.

SHE DIDN'T WADDLE her way to freedom.

She wanted to. Boy, did she ever. But she couldn't make a break for it without upsetting her sisters, and so she climbed—at a much slower pace than usual thanks to the layers of fabric—into her beat-up Chevy pickup and followed the line of trucks and SUVs headed out to the Gunner Ranch where the reception was being held.

At the reception, she kept as wide a distance from her mother as possible, and ignored the phone in her pocketbook that vibrated every few minutes with a new text. The most startling of which?

How would you like to be my new bartender?

Ugh.

The last thing she wanted was to serve beers for the rest of her life. She'd spent the past few years dressing like her sisters and putting up a front to stay off her mother's radar, while secretly pursuing her culinary degree. She'd even managed to stash away a sizable nest egg to tide her over through an internship. She wanted out of here, a chance to live her own life, to fulfill her own dreams.

But first she had to make it through finals in two weeks without losing her focus.

Fat chance if she ended up slinging Coronas side by side with Raylene Barbie.

She ignored yet another text, finished taking the mandatory pictures and darted off toward the buffet line before her mother could pin her down.

She squeezed through the throng of wedding guests stuffed into the massive white tent where the reception was being held. A country band played a soft, twangy version of Willie Nelson's *Always on My Mind*.

Seriously? Forget Miranda Lambert's ballsy *Gunpowder and Lead*—the Barbie theme song. Her sisters really had gone off the deep end.

All the more reason to cut and run.

Now.

She bypassed the buffet and headed through a nearby tent that had been set up to house the food. After a quick glance to make sure no one was watching, she darted into the tent, and nearly collided with a waiter carrying a tray of crab cakes.

She paused to snag a sample before murmuring "Sorry," and turned to make her way through the massive square-shaped kitchen. Burners and stoves lined the outer perimeter. The inner area was a maze of preparation tables. People clustered here and there, busily arranging everything from trays of speared shrimp to platters of cold vegetables and gourmet cheeses. There wasn't a hot wing or a fried pickle in sight—none of the usual fare that her mother offered up at the honky-tonk. Even more proof that Raylene was, at this moment, going into shock from the one-eighty her world had taken.

Her mother wasn't much for gourmet cuisine, which was why Nikki had been lying about taking a pole-dancing class in Austin three times a week. In reality, she made the hour-long drive to attend an advanced gourmet-entrée class to work on her very own twist to the traditional beef Wellington that was sure to win its way onto the menu in one of Houston's finest.

Fat chance now.

Her life was ruined. Her dream over. Her future tanked.

She fought down a wave of tears and bypassed a woman in a white chef's hat who fed slices of cake onto individual crystal plates. The sweet, sugary aroma teased her nostrils, promising a temporary distraction.

Forget that. She needed alcohol.

She snagged an open bottle of wine from a nearby tray and took a long swig. Her sisters had gone all out. Forget a box of Pinot Grigio from the local Piggly Wiggly. She was drinking an aged White Zinfandel that slid down her throat with a smooth sweetness that eased the panic for a few seconds and slowed her pounding heart.

Another long drink and she left the service tent behind and headed for the barn that sat several yards away.

A little distance and a lot of wine and maybe, just maybe, she could figure out some way to deal with the disaster that was fast becoming her life.

She could spike her mother's favorite moonshine three times a week with a couple of Ambien. That, along with the one-hundred-and-eighty proof, would surely be enough to knock her mother out so she could finish the class, ace the exam and get her degree.

And, more than likely, cause some serious brain damage to the one woman who'd endured twenty hours and thirty-three minutes of labor on her behalf.

Of course, the moonshine wasn't any more an option than the Ambien. She didn't have a prescription, nor did she have any of Big Earl Jessup's famous White Lightning. The old man could barely remember his name, much less his prized recipe.

Another all-important fact which had Raylene acting even more desperate. She had over twenty different drinks on her bar menu that featured Big Earl's classic moonshine. A secret weapon that upped her take at least twenty percent on any given Saturday night and gave her an edge over the bigger, flash-

ier bars popping up along the main interstate. Raylene's place had long since been a draw not only to
the locals, but to the endless string of tourists that
passed through Lost Gun. And all because of her
Texas Lightning Margarita.

Sure, she told everyone, particularly Sheriff
Hooker, that she used an aged tequila, but the folks in
Lost Gun knew the taste of old Earl's premium-grade
liquor well enough to know better. And they talked.
And that talk lured the tourists. And the tourists kept
Raylene in black leather bustiers and salted peanuts.
And Raylene's business was the only thing that kept
her too busy to focus on Nikki's personal life.

Was being the key word.

The smell of hay and leather surrounded her as
she fled deep into the massive barn that sat at the
far edge of the property, bottle in hand, panic flut-
tering in her chest.

She took another long, much-needed drink and
tried to think of something good. Something calm.
Something monotonous. Like chopping Vidalia on-
ions or whipping fresh, scented cream or kneading
a blue-cheese brioche—

The thought stalled as she heard the clink of sil-
verware against a plate.

Her gaze went to the ladder that led to the overhead rafters. Another *clink* and she knew she wasn't
alone in her misery.

Somebody was up there.

Kicking off the hated satin shoes, she mounted the ladder and made her way up to the second floor. Wood groaned as she reached the last step and topped the landing. Her gaze went to the far end where the monstrous shutters had been pushed open and moonlight spilled through the large square. Framed in the opening was a man perched atop a hay bale.

The man.

The object of way too many fantasies over the years.

But then she was only human, and Cole Chisholm was a one-hundred-percent, certified beefcake.

A small lantern hung nearby, casting a pale yellow glow that fell across his face as she neared where he sat.

He held a plate of half-eaten white cake in one hand and fork in the other. A black tuxedo jacket accented his broad shoulders. His crisp white shirt hugged the strong column of his throat and provided a stark contrast against his deeply tanned skin. Light brown hair streaked with gold hung past his collar and framed his strong face.

Hay crunched beneath her feet. He lifted his head and swiveled toward her.

Familiar violet eyes collided with hers and his expression went from irritation to pure delight in one fast, furious heartbeat, as if he were covering up his initial dismay. His full lips curved into a grin. A dimple cut into his shadowed cheek. His gaze glittered in the dim barn light.

A wave of heat went through her. Her breath caught and her tummy hollowed out, and for a split second, she forgot that Cole Chisholm wasn't her type.

With the wine numbing her senses and her mother a safe distance away, the only thing she could think was that he was the most scrumptious thing she'd seen all day.

And boy, oh, boy, would she like to take a bite.

But then he opened his mouth, his deep Southern drawl sweet and dripping with charm, and the moment faded as she remembered why she'd opted for culinary school in lieu of burning the midnight oil at the honky-tonk.

Because it kept her far, far away from men like Cole Chisholm. The sexy, charming, let's-get-naked-in-the-backseat types that oozed sex appeal and sweet compliments. The ones who were here today, gone tomorrow. The exact type her mother specialized in.

His sensual lips hinted at the most heart-stopping grin. "I knew it was just a matter of time before some pretty young thing followed me up here." He patted the seat next to him. "Plant one right here, sugar. I'm all yours."

2

COLE UNGER CHISHOLM wasn't the kind of man to let a little misfortune ruin his entire day.

Hell, no. He was an optimist. A the-beer-bottle-is-half-full kind of guy. He just dodged the bullets of bad luck that fate aimed at him and kept moving.

The ordinary .22 kind. One shot. One hit.

But damned if it didn't seem as if he was dodging a spray of buckshot tonight.

Sure, they'd found the last of the money out at Big Earl's, but it would be another week and a half before they could actually turn it over to the sheriff. It seemed the man had been called out of town on a statewide manhunt that had started in Beaumont and was currently making its way toward Brownsville. All available law enforcement within a hundred-mile radius had been summoned to the scene. Since the most action Sheriff Hooker usually saw was the occasional Friday night drunk, he'd been more than ready to pack up his car and head for the real action, leaving his deputies in charge. Tweedledee and Tweedledum. Needless to say, Jesse had decided to wait until the sheriff returned to hand over the bank-heist money. Which meant Cole would not be rolling out of town tonight.

Even worse, he was stuck at the wedding for the next several hours until Jimmy and Jake tossed the garter and headed for the airport. Three more freakin' *hours*. Why, Millie Van Horten had already cornered him twice to ask him to dance. Shae Rigby had brought him not one, but two slices of cake. And Jamie Lee Milburn had offered to give him a back rub.

And the really bad part was that he'd been this close to taking her up on her offer. His shoulders hurt like a sonofabitch after all that digging and a few magic fingers might actually make things bearable.

Thankfully, he'd come to his senses and told her he'd already promised his own back rub to Mary Lou Canter and Sharon Jenkins. And Christie Somerville. The idea? To show her what a disreputable guy he was and discourage her.

Like hell.

The more he played the wild and wicked player, the more determined each woman became to be the one to rope him in. It made sense. He was smack-dab in the middle of a wedding, for heaven's sake. Every man in his right mind knew that women got a little crazy at weddings.

They saw the cake and bam, they wanted to be right there, cutting into the decadent layers, feeding it to the man of their dreams—that is, the nearest available bachelor.

Since his two brothers and every other member of the notorious Lost Boys were now officially spoken for, Cole was the only one still on the market.

The biggest catch this side of the Rio Grande or so the local About Town reporter had just scribbled on her pad during an interview a few minutes ago. No doubt tomorrow's headline in the local Sunday paper. As if things weren't bad enough already. Once tomorrow hit, he would be even more sought after than a hot, fresh-from-the-oven biscuit at a no-carbs convention. Every woman in town would be trying to drag him to the weekly church picnic.

While he liked a good barbecue as much as the next guy, he had no intention of showing up with any woman. That would be like hanging a sign on his back. *Ready, willing and marriageable*. He was none of the above, especially with less than four weeks until the national saddle-bronc championship. He was *this* close to winning another title—*the* title that would put him in the record books and solidify a spot in the saddle-bronc Hall of Fame—and he didn't need any distractions. Even more, he wasn't the marrying kind any more than his no-good, no-account father had been. The difference was, Cole had no problem admitting it.

Not that anyone seemed to believe it.

Despite the fact that he'd spent the past hour doing his damnedest to beef up his bad boy image and kiss goodbye his husband potential. He'd sucked down a few shots and danced it up with as many women as possible. But then his calves had started aching and his stomach had grumbled, and so he was here.

And so was she.

Nikki Barbie wasn't wearing her usual black leather miniskirt or tight T-shirt, but she still looked every bit as sexy. She had long blond hair, bright blue eyes and a curvaceous body that did the Barbie name justice. Dark eye makeup emphasized her blue eyes and gave her that "come and do me" look. Pale pink lipstick plumped her already full lips. Everything about her screamed sex, which suited him to a T.

When he had his game face on, that is.

But he wasn't beefing up his image at the moment. He was hiding from it.

Cole pasted on his most charming grin and hid the cake plate behind his back.

"Hey there, sugar." He summoned his best panty-dropping drawl. "Nice dress." He winked and went the extra mile to lay it on thick. "Or it would be if there was a lot less of it."

"In your dreams."

He grinned. "Every night."

IF ONLY.

The thought struck Nikki just as Cole smiled again, and heat spiraled through her.

A crazy reaction considering Nikki was an ice queen when it came to men like Cole Chisholm. He dropped lines faster than a cow dropped patties. She knew it because she dropped a few of her own when she was out in public. Just to keep her image in check and her mother at arm's length.

But it was useless flirtation that didn't really mean anything, and no way should she actually be blushing because of it.

Because of him.

"Are you eating cake?" Nikki noticed the speck of frosting at the corner of his mouth.

He looked as if he wanted to deny it, but instead he finally shrugged. His right arm came around, revealing a crystal plate and a half-eaten piece of fluffy white cake. "Nothing wrong with a man enjoying a good dessert."

Her gaze shifted to what looked like a large glass of chocolate milk sitting on the hay bale next to him. She arched an eyebrow. "A Back Burner? A Brown

Cow? A Russian Six Shot?" She ticked off a few alcoholic drink possibilities because this was Cole Chisholm, of all people.

Wild.

Wicked.

Reckless.

He grinned. "You know it."

"Which one?"

"The first one."

Something about the way he said the words roused her suspicion. She stepped toward him, grabbed the glass before he could snatch it out of her reach and lifted it to her lips. "You're drinking plain old chocolate milk," she said after a quick whiff.

"Says you. I've got a ton of Everclear in there, sugar. That's why you can't smell it."

"No, you don't." Understanding dawned. "You're hiding in here so that no one will see you drinking chocolate milk and eating plain old wedding cake."

"Darlin', there's nothing plain or old about this cake."

"It's vanilla. No filling. Plain."

"And just what would you have done differently?"

She shrugged. "I don't know. Maybe a chocolate ganache with a raspberry-liquor filling. A little crème fraîche on the side."

"You're a food snob."

"I am not." She averted her gaze. "I like a plain

old piece of cake as much as the next person. I'm just not hungry right now." Her gaze met his again. "Stop trying to change the subject."

"Which is?"

"You're hiding."

"Says you." He glanced past her. "No one saw you come out here, did they?"

"You *are* hiding."

"It's called self-preservation. There's something going around out there and I don't intend to catch it."

She arched an eyebrow. "Strep? Flu? Meningitis?"

"Mary Lou Harwell." He shook his head. "She won't leave me alone."

"She's young and nice and pretty. Trust me, you could have worse problems."

"She wants me to father her children."

She shrugged. "No one's perfect."

He grinned and her stomach hollowed out again. "So what's the big deal with the cake and the milk? I could see if you were eating bean sprouts or quiche or something equally unmanly, but it's just cake."

"It's cake and whole chocolate milk. As in *whole-*some." His mouth drew into a thin line and he shook his head, as if he'd already said more than he wanted to.

"And Cole Chisholm can't be wholesome?" she heard herself ask. As if she didn't already know the answer. She'd spent more than one night with a beer bottle full of ginger ale back at the honky-tonk.

Cole didn't seem as if he wanted to talk, but then he finally shrugged. "I've got an image to think of." He walked back over to the hay bale and retrieved his plate.

"So chase the cake with a few whiskey shots and you're good to go."

He looked at her as if she'd grown two heads. "A man can't eat cake with whiskey. Do you know how awful that would taste?"

"Apparently you've never had a good whiskey sauce poured over buttered pound cake." Did she just say that out loud? "Not that I've ever tried anything like that. I'm more of a Twinkie girl." Her hands tightened around the wine bottle and she barely resisted the urge to take another swig. But she'd already destroyed enough brain cells. Otherwise, she wouldn't be spouting nonsense about whiskey sauce and crème fraîche, or any other dead giveaway that she was more than just a bar cook at the local honky-tonk. No, if she'd been thinking clearly, she would have kept her mouth shut. Even more, she would have turned on her heel and on Cole without so much as a backward glance.

At the moment, however, she couldn't *not* look at him as he forked some cake and took a bite. The speck of sweet, decadent frosting still sat at the corner of his mouth as he chewed.

Nikki had the sudden urge to cross the few feet between them and taste the sweet icing. Her mouth watered and she tightened her fingers against the fierce hunger.

This is totally whacked. He's not your type, remember? Even more, she had a refined palate. She'd sworn off any and all nongourmet when she'd registered for her first culinary class two years ago. She didn't do cake. And she certainly didn't do men like Cole Chisholm.

Unfortunately, her hormones had a very short memory and they couldn't seem to get past the warmth in his smile and the twinkle in his violet eyes and the fact that she'd been totally celibate for much too long—since her one and only one-night stand with Mitch Schaeffer. *The* one-night stand that had simply confirmed what she'd already known in her heart. He'd been her first and her last.

Because Nikki wanted more than a few hours of hot, breath-stealing sex. She wanted a real boyfriend. A man to bring her flowers and make her breakfast and make her feel like more than just a sex object.

Not right now, of course. The last thing she needed was to tie herself down.

She had a future waiting for her, one well beyond the city limits of her desperately small town.

But someday…

Someday she would meet a good man, a faithful, honest and true sort who didn't spend his Friday nights lighting it up at the local honky-tonk. She saw too many of those every weekend and it didn't bode well for a healthy, monogamous relationship. No, when she settled down, it would be with a solid, dependable, *tame* man.

Cole Chisholm, with his womanizing reputation and his "here today, gone tomorrow" mentality, did not make the grade. Even if he did like whole chocolate milk.

Still, wrong or not, Cole Chisholm did smell terribly nice. Her nostrils flared and the butterflies in her stomach did a few somersaults.

She drew a deep breath and tried to ignore the crazy tilt to the floor. "I think I need to sit down."

Cole grinned and patted the seat next to him. "Take a load off."

She hesitated. "I'm not having sex with you."

"See?" He held up the glass of milk. "I told you this stuff kills the old image."

"I'm not having sex with you because I've had way too much sex tonight and I'm really tired."

"Is that so?"

She shrugged. "A girl has to have some down time. Not that I don't want to have sex with you. I totally would if my feet weren't hurting so bad." She wasn't sure why she kept rambling except that with the music playing in the distance and his close proximity there seemed something oddly surreal about the moment. "I'd be all over you."

"Ditto," he murmured, downing a huge swallow of milk. He took a bite of cake and his eyes closed as if savoring the medley of flavors.

"It's got real vanilla bean," she blurted.

His eyes opened and collided with hers. "What?"

"The cake. That faint hint of flavor is vanilla bean. It's April and Crystal's favorite. They commissioned a baker in Austin to do it." Even though Nikki could have totally nailed it herself. Her flavors had all been there, but she'd been nervous about her decorating skills. We're talking a wedding cake, for heaven's sake. That, and the last thing she needed was to tell the world that she'd been cooking up more in the honky-tonk's kitchen than crispy fried pickles. "I'm working on my culinary degree," she heard herself add when he kept staring at her.

What was she doing?

She wasn't supposed to be blurting out her life story. She had an image to protect. A facade to perpetuate. She had to keep her game face on.

In front of a man drinking whole chocolate milk?

The truth registered and while she knew he was all about lovin' and leavin', he wasn't going anywhere at the moment. No, he was looking at her as if he wanted to hear what she had to say. As if he wasn't half as surprised as he was interested.

"I didn't know you were going to culinary school."

"No one does." When he arched an eyebrow, she added, "My mother would freak. She thinks women have fought too hard to get out of the kitchen. She hates to cook. She watched my grandmother cook and clean herself into an early grave and she swore she wouldn't make the same mistake. Cooking is right up there with being barefoot and pregnant." A big no-no in Raylene's book. Which was why Nikki and her sisters had grown up eating fast food.

Her mother would never understand her career choice any more than she would accept the fact that Nikki was breaking Barbie tradition and leaving home after finals.

Especially now that her sisters were married and Nikki was the only one left.

The enormity of the situation pressed down on her and she slumped on the hay bale next to Cole Chisholm. "What the hell am I going to do?" She swallowed against the huge lump rising in her throat. "I've got finals in two weeks. I need to concentrate. To focus. I can't focus with my mother all over me, which means I need to figure out a way to get her off my back. And all because my sisters tied the knot."

"I hear ya. I'm ready to pack up and leave today, but I can't. I've got business here in town with my brothers and I'm stuck for at least a week. Meanwhile there are at least two dozen women hot on my heels."

A smile tugged at her lips. "Only two dozen, huh?"

He grinned. "Give or take a few."

Nikki wasn't sure if it was the wine or the warmth of Cole's hard body that sparked the next thought. Maybe a little of both. Regardless, an idea rooted and she found herself smiling.

"I should get married," she told him. "My mother's given up on Crystal and April because they did. If I jumped ship, too, and married some man that she totally disapproves of—which is basically every man—then she wouldn't have any reason to hold out hope." Nikki's gaze shifted to Cole with his wicked good looks and his charming smile and his empty glass of chocolate milk. "I've got an idea that might save us both."

3

"I DO," NIKKI SAID a half hour later as she stood in the far corner of the monstrous wedding tent and faced Cole.

Crystal and April had already left with their grooms in a flurry of bubbles to catch a plane to Hawaii for their honeymoons, and so Nikki had lucked out. She wouldn't have to explain anything to her sisters tonight.

Likewise, Cole's brothers had already left with their fiancées. Only a handful of guests remained and a few reporters. They stood on the sidelines, snapping pictures of the spontaneous wedding between Lost Gun's hottest bachelor and the town's most notorious bad girl.

Now Cole was officially off the market, which meant every single female in town would stop gunning for him. Likewise, Raylene Barbie would be so horrified that her youngest daughter had done the unthinkable, that she would stop sending texts and badgering her about the family business.

Nikki could have some peace to focus on finishing her degree and Cole could spend the next week or so in town without having a horde of women breathing down his neck and bringing him potluck. It was extreme, but it would actually work.

After Nikki's proposition and Cole's acceptance, they'd ironed out the details of their "marriage."

An arrangement in name only since they didn't actually have a license, nor did they intend to get one.

Not that anyone else knew that.

No, in the eyes of everyone in Lost Gun, their marriage would be legal and binding.

For the next few weeks, that is.

Until Cole aced the championship in Vegas and secured himself a place in the history books and Nikki took her final exams. Then they would go their separate ways and leak the word that they'd split. Nikki would head to Houston for her internship and Cole would bask in the glow of his sixth championship buckle.

Until then, they would play the happily wedded couple right here in Lost Gun.

And I now pronounce you husband and wife...

"You may now kiss the bride."

The minute the words were out, panic rushed

through Nikki, along with a flutter of anticipation. While she'd thought through most of the details, she hadn't counted on the kiss.

No biggie. She was the resident bad girl. She kissed men in her sleep and she didn't get uptight over it. Or weak in the knees.

Especially weak in the knees.

Cole was just another in a long line of many.

That's what she told herself. The problem? It wasn't true. She'd had all of a handful of kisses in her day, even though the men's bathroom wall over at the honky-tonk would argue the opposite. And they said women liked to gossip? Men were worse, constantly wagging their tongues to feed their egos even though there was little truth to any of it. She hadn't made out with the entire offensive line back in high school or gone to third base with every ranch hand down at the Circle J.

For the first time, she found herself wishing that she had so that her hands wouldn't be trembling quite so much as this particular moment.

Nikki closed her eyes as Cole's lips touched hers. Quick. Meaningless. That's all this was. He would plant one on her and then it would be over and done with. Curtain drawn. Elvis has left the building.

But then her lips softened under the sudden pressure of his mouth. His tongue swept her bottom lip and slipped past to deepen the connection.

He pulled her closer, his hands at the base of her spine, burning through the thin material of her dress and stirring her deprived hormones.

The chemistry between them was instant and explosive and she couldn't help herself. She knew this was all a farce, but she kissed him back anyway.

In the interest of putting on a really good show, of course.

No way did she buckle because it just felt so freakin' *good*.

No. Way.

She slid her hands up his chest, her palms flat against the stiff material of his jacket until she reached the solid warmth of his neck. Her fingers curled around, holding him close.

Okay, so maybe it felt a little good.

The floor fell away as she leaned into him. His warmth overwhelmed her. His scent filled her nostrils and made her heart pound and—

"Nicole Renee Barbie!" Her mother's voice shattered the passionate haze surrounding Nikki and Cole and her eyes popped open. "What in tarnation do you think you're doing?"

She whirled to see Raylene walking toward them, her latest fling—a trucker named Dale Something-or-other she'd picked up last night at the bar—hot on her heels.

"Kissing a man."

"I'm not talking about the kissing. I'm talking about this." She motioned to the bouquet in Nikki's hands and old Judge Collins who'd been napping in the corner while his wife talked the kitchen out of a plate of leftovers when Nikki had snagged him to do the ceremony. "You didn't just do what I think you did."

"These fine youngsters are now happily married," the judge announced, stifling a yawn. "Mother." He motioned to the woman standing with a plate in her hands. "My work here is done. Time to call it a night."

"Thanks so much." Cole shook the man's hand. "I'll settle up with you first thing tomorrow."

"Don't worry about it." The judge's wife waved him off. "He won't even remember it. We're just happy we could be a part of such a wonderful occasion. Marshall doesn't get to officiate too often on account of he has trouble remembering all the words."

"He did just fine tonight," Cole assured the woman. "Just fine. Isn't that right, sugar?" He turned to Nikki, but she was too busy looking at Raylene.

The older woman shook her head, her cheeks a bright red. "No, no, you couldn't have." Denial gripped her expression, as if the Dallas Cowboys had just lost the Super Bowl and she had a wad of cash riding on the game. "No way did you just saddle yourself to some low-life, snake-in-the-grass *man*."

Before Nikki could speak, Cole stepped around her and caught her mother in a gigantic bear hug. "Don't think of me as just any old snake-in-the-grass, Mama Barbie. We're family now. That makes me *your* snake-in-the-grass." And then he planted a huge smack on her cheek.

4

NIKKI CLIMBED INTO the backseat of one of the stretch limousines that had lingered behind to take the out-of-town wedding guests back to the local motel and focused all of her attention on trying to ignore the man who climbed in behind her.

Her husband.

The thought rooted in her mind as the driver tipped his hat before rolling the security window into place. The engine roared to life and the massive vehicle rumbled down the road, away from the festivities.

Not that theirs was a real marriage, but still. At the moment, it almost felt real with the kiss at the altar and the plush limousine and, well, it *was* their wedding night.

And she was feeling uncommonly good thanks to half a bottle of wine, one hell of a spectacular kiss and the fact that her mother had turned on her heel and marched off in the opposite direction after Cole's big display of familial affection.

"I can't believe she bought it."

"Did you see Sally Fisk and Tara Lawrence?" He grinned. "They were texting before we even said our 'I dos.' Half the town has to know about this by now." His grin widened. "This just might work."

"It will work," she said with more confidence than she'd felt in a long, long time.

He was so close and so strong and he smelled so good—like sweet vanilla-bean wedding cake and while her palate had graduated to more sophisticated flavors, she found herself with a sudden craving for something simple. Tasty. Satisfying.

"Yep, I think this is just what the ole doc ordered." He half turned. A grin tilted the corner of his mouth as he pinned her with a gaze.

Nikki's heart stalled and she couldn't help herself.

She leaned forward and touched her lips to his. It was nothing short of explosive. The chemistry ignited and mushroomed, and what started as a subtle press of mouths soon morphed into a deep, urgent, delicious probing of tongues.

No, no, no, a voice whispered. This was too fast, too soon. At the same time, she'd wanted to kiss him like this since she'd been a seventh grader, sitting at the Dairy Freeze, watching him feed a banana split to her oldest sister. She'd been too much younger back then, but now... Now the age difference didn't matter. They were both adults.

Married adults.

Caution melted away in the face of so much heat, and arousal washed through Nikki from her head to the tips of her bright pink toenails. The pulsing awareness started in her scalp and spread through her body, pausing at every major erogenous zone. Her nipples tightened and hardened. Pressure hummed between her legs. Her thighs quivered. Her heart pounded as loud and as fast as the drummer for Buckcherry, and her blood rushed at an alarming rate.

"We probably shouldn't be doing this," she murmured.

"Then again, if anyone should be doing it, it's us." Cole's hand found its way under her dress and swept a burning path up the inside of her thigh.

"True enough," she breathed as his finger traced the lace edge of her panties before dipping underneath.

His finger ran back and forth, his callused skin arousing Nikki's sensitized flesh. Back and forth. Up and...oh, boy.

He pushed into her and she gasped. She wiggled, pivoting her hips, desperate to feel him deeper and harder and... There. Just like that. And that. And—oh, wow—*that*...

His lips left her mouth to blaze a trail down her throat to her pulse beat. He rasped the tip of his tongue against her skin and worked his finger inside her body. A moan vibrated from her throat. Cole caught the sound with his mouth and devoured her in another luscious kiss.

Suddenly, the limo swerved and the driver's muttered curse penetrated the haze of desire that enveloped them. Not that the driver could actually see anything with the privacy window firmly in place. But it was still obvious from the panting and moaning going on that Cole was doing something, and that Nikki was enjoying it and—

The thought scattered in a rush of desire as he pushed deep inside.

She relished his deep, thrusting touch for a few more delicious moments before he pulled out of her completely. The tips of his fingers skimmed her swollen flesh as he caught her thigh. She trembled as he urged her leg up and over his lap until she straddled him. They faced one another, her dress bunched around her waist.

Cole's violet gaze drilled into hers, his eyes dilated with hunger and a deep appreciation. Warmth bubbled inside her, a feeling that might have spooked her if she hadn't been so hot and bothered in the first place.

Barbie women didn't do bubbling warmth. Or

soft fuzzies. Or any of those girly feelings that undermined even the most determined woman when it came to men. They didn't let themselves get involved in the emotional aspect of sex because that would only make it harder to walk away the next day. And they always walked away. They had a reputation to maintain, after all.

Not that Nikki had done a lot of walking away the morning after. Because there hadn't been much sex the night before. Her sisters perpetuated the reputation with their carousing ways, and so all Nikki had ever had to do was dress the part and flirt her ass off and bam, she'd been part of the one-night-stand club.

But she'd never actually gotten good at it.

She might be a Barbie in name, but she didn't have near the expertise her sisters possessed when it came to pleasuring the opposite sex. Sure, she'd tried. With a basketball player named David. He'd asked her to the senior prom, but before they'd even made it to the dance, he'd had her in the backseat for a little pre-dance action.

She'd given in and then instead of taking her to the prom, he'd made some lame excuse about having to go home for an emergency. He'd dropped her off at her door so fast she'd had whiplash. He'd gone on to brag about it, but he'd never come back for seconds. No late-night calls to hook up. Nothing.

Meanwhile, when one of her sisters had given it

up, she hadn't been able to get rid of the guy. Men had chased after them mercilessly. Because her sisters had been great in the sack.

Nikki? Not so much. Which wasn't all that much of a problem in itself since she was much too busy to worry over a bunch of sex-crazed guys chasing after her. She had a career to think of. Goals to achieve. Even more, she had a sizable vibrator that did the job just fine and didn't leave her angsting about a follow-up phone call.

And so she stuck to flirting to keep up her image rather than actually hooking up.

A fact that slipped her mind at that moment because she'd had a little too much wine and Cole felt too good and she wanted him too much.

As if he read her mind, his strong hands cupped her bare bottom and he worked her against the rock-hard bulge pressing tight against his jeans. The friction was incredible and stirring. Her head fell back and her eyes closed as pleasure ripped through her.

She shimmied her hips and spread her legs even wider, settling more fully on top of him. He let loose a low growl and leaned forward, his hot mouth going to the plump cleavage pushing against the low neckline of her dress. His tongue traced the edge of the material before he reached his hand up to grasp the edge of the material. He was just about to pull it down and free her aching breast when an all-important fact registered.

Nikki wasn't clutching at his shoulders to keep from swaying to the side anymore. They were sitting stock still, the limo engine idling, the driver waiting. And probably wondering.

"We're here," she breathed.

Cole's hand stilled as his gaze met hers. They stared at each other for a long moment, their breaths coming in quick, frantic gulps.

"We sure are." He sounded disappointed.

Until reality seemed to hit, and then it was as if someone lit a fire under them. She scrambled from his lap and pushed open the door to step out onto the pavement while he followed her out.

The large building that housed the honky-tonk sat dark and quiet, closed for tonight's wedding. She picked up her steps and headed around the side to the stairs leading to the small apartment on the second floor. Her mother had once lived in the apartment when she'd first opened the place, but when Nikki's grandmother had died, she'd moved into the small house that sat a few blocks over. And so the apartment had been left to Nikki and her sisters.

Now that Crystal and April were married, Nikki had the place all to herself.

Cole followed and soon Nikki fumbled with her key for a few moments before Cole stepped up behind her and wrapped his arms around her waist. His long, lean fingers closed over hers, and he steadied her long enough to slide the key into the lock. Metal clicked and hinges creaked and then they were inside. The door slammed behind them and before she could draw a breath, he whirled her around and pulled her into his arms.

He kissed her, his tongue delving deep as he pulled her close. Her thighs quivered and her bosom heaved and she came dangerously close to fainting from the desire swamping her. But this was too good to miss and she wasn't about to forfeit what was surely to be a really incredible orgasm.

Her first with an actual man.

She reached for the waistband of his pants as he reached behind for the hooks on her dress. They both worked at the clothes until all the pieces had been pulled away. The nightmare bridesmaid's dress landed in a heap somewhere across the room. The matching slip slapped the far wall. Nikki feared her corset-like bra would put up a fight, but Cole quickly demonstrated why he was the hottest catch in town. A few movements of his deft fingers and the bra fell away. Soon she was completely naked.

Likewise, Cole's clothes followed hers. His jacket hit the floor along with his belt and jeans. Buttons popped and she shoved the shirt down his arms and sent the white material flying in the opposite direction. She paused only to discover whether he went for boxers, briefs, or let it all hang out—crisp white boxer briefs, just for the record—before shoving the elastic waistband down and freeing a massive erection.

She wanted to look, but everything seemed so fuzzy and surreal and desperate. She threw herself against him. Her body went flush against his as bare skin met bare skin. His lips found hers again. He kissed her as he swept her into his arms and started for the bedroom.

There was just something about the way his mouth ate at her lips and his tongue tangled with hers, stroking this way and that, up and down, deeper and stronger, that took her breath away. She'd never met a man who kissed with such passion and intensity. As if he liked it. As if he liked *her*.

The last thought rooted in her mind as he tumbled her back onto her full-size bed. Her dog, Sweet Cheeks, who'd been curled up on her pillow, jumped to the floor with a loud, surprised yelp. She then let loose a grumpy growl before scurrying off toward the walk-in closet that housed her doggy pillow.

Cole's body covered Nikki's and settled between her legs. He reached to grip her buttocks and tilt her up, to ready her for what was about to happen.

Sex.

Convenient sex.

They were stuck in a relationship together, however temporary, and so they might as well make the most of it.

And if convenient sex turns into bad sex?

The question whispered through her mind and she tried to ignore it. It would be good. It had to be good.

And you've got the track record to prove that, right?

"Stop," she blurted in that next instant. "I, um, think we should put on the brakes."

He stiffened and pulled away to stare down at her. "Why?"

Yeah, why?

"Because we don't want to complicate our relationship, however temporary, with sex. This is supposed to be a marriage in name only. We didn't lay out any ground rules for getting busy."

"Maybe we should. I mean, I've got needs and you've got needs, right?"

"Oh, yeah, sure. Lots." She fought to hide the anxiety spiking inside her and forced her hands to stop holding on to the hard muscles of his shoulders. "Tons. But should we really be wasting our time on sex when what we both really need is to focus?" *Bad hands*. She balled her fingers and tried to remember every reason she shouldn't be touching him right now. "That's why we're doing this in the first place. To kill all the distractions and focus on what's really important. Not that you can tell anyone that. We have to keep this just between us, otherwise the entire town will figure out it's not for real." She scrambled out from beneath him. "I've got to make béarnaise sauce for Monday's class and I've never made béarnaise sauce. I really need to practice. And you should be riding a bronc or something, shouldn't you?"

"It's one o'clock in the morning. I don't bronc bust at this crazy hour. I usually sleep."

"Good idea. You take this bed. I'll just crash on the sofa when I finish up with the sauce." And then she retreated into the safety of her kitchen and left Cole Chisholm alone in her bedroom.

No doubt thinking that she was a nutcase.

Better certifiable than a total disappointment in bed.

The last thing she needed was for Cole to know the truth—that Nikki Barbie was a fake. That her carnal knowledge amounted to zilch and she couldn't come close to living up to her name. She knew zilch when it came to heating up the bedroom.

No, the only room she knew her way around was the kitchen. Which was where she kept herself for the next few hours as she tried to forget all about the naked man lying in her bed.

5

WHAT THE HELL was wrong with him?

Cole watched the spray of neon play across the ceiling courtesy of the honky-tonk's buzzing neon sign that sat just outside the window.

He wasn't supposed to jump her bones in the limo, or here in her bedroom. And he sure as hell wasn't supposed to be so damned tense. Uptight. *Ready.*

To march into the kitchen, sling her over his shoulder and haul her back to bed.

She was right.

They needed to remember why they were doing this and keep their relationship strictly platonic. That's what he'd fully intended.

But then she'd smiled at him in the limo and leaned forward, and he'd forgotten every good intention.

He hadn't expected his stomach to hollow out at

the sight of her smile, but it had. It wasn't as if he was a damned stranger when it came to women. He'd had more than his share, particularly over the past few years since he'd nailed championship after championship. He didn't go all hard at the sight of a pair of long legs, or a nice ass, or even a substantial pair of breasts. And he sure as hell didn't get all hot and bothered over a woman's smile.

Not when he was this close to a win.

No, he saved the cutting loose for the right time. The right place. The right woman. Namely one who would be on her way before the sun came up.

But Nikki's lips were just so full and lush, her teeth straight and white. And she had this dimple that cut into her upper cheek and softened her entire expression. A sight that he remembered all too well, though the effect was much more potent now.

The first time he'd seen it had been years ago. Back when he was in middle school. She'd been in kindergarten back then and a student at the nearby elementary school. She'd walked a similar route home from school with her sisters and, of course, he'd always tagged along after Crystal. But one day Crystal had been home sick and April had stayed after school for detention, and Nikki had been all by her lonesome.

She'd been scared navigating the route home by herself, but then she'd seen him. Her eyes had spar-

kled and her lips had parted and she'd given him a
smile that had made him feel like a superhero rather
than the son of the town lowlife.

Her sisters had been back on duty the next day
and he'd gone back to panting after Crystal, but he'd
never forgotten the look. The memory had gotten
him through more than one bad moment over the
years. Even so, he'd never thought to see it up close
and personal again.

But then she'd been right there in front of him and
she'd smiled and...well, here he was, nursing a hard-
on that was damn near painful.

He thought of closing his eyes and trying to get
some sleep, but with her scent still ripe around him
and her soft, flower-print sheets brushing his skin,
he knew there was about a popsicle's chance in hell
of that. No, better to get the inevitable over with.

He pulled out his cell phone. It had only been two
hours since they'd left the wedding, but he'd already
had five missed calls from Jesse. News traveled fast
in a small town. Bad news even faster, and the two
wildest broncs on the single circuit definitely con-
stituted bad news.

"Would you mind telling me what the hell you
were thinking tonight?" Jesse demanded the minute he answered Cole's call. Without waiting for a
reply, his brother rushed on, "You've pulled a lot of

stunts before, but this takes the cake. I thought you liked being unattached. I thought you thrived on it."

"Maybe I'm tired of it. Maybe I'm trying to clean up my image and walk the straight and narrow."

"By marrying *Nikki Barbie?*"

"Okay, so maybe I'm trying to reinforce my image. I'm a bad guy, Jess. I grew up on the wrong side of the tracks. Hell, I grew up *on* the tracks."

"You're preaching to the choir, bro."

"Then I don't have to tell you that I'm hardly a decent catch for any of the women in this town."

"I don't know about that. There's one woman here who would argue with you."

"Gracie doesn't count. She's practically my family. She's supposed to think nice things about her soon-to-be brother-in-law. But you know what I'm talking about, Jesse. You know the shit everyone talked about us when we were kids."

"And I know that half that crap wasn't even close to the truth."

"But the other half was. We put up with a lot when we were growing up and it changed us. We had to do things that no kid should. It made us hard. Wild."

"We survived and we're here now. Better off, and better men."

"Just because things are easier now doesn't mean we've calmed down any." He heard Gracie in the background and he added, "At least I haven't calmed down. You're whipped. We all know that."

"I wouldn't be throwing stones. You're well on your way based on what I heard tonight."

"Like hell. I'm a maverick, bro. And I intend to stay that way. The sooner the women in this town realize that, the better. Not that it matters now. They'll have to stop chasing because I'm officially off the market."

"And there it is. The real reason for tonight."

"Hey, I was going to hit the road, but now I've got to stick around for who knows how long. I had to do something. I've got Vegas coming up in three weeks. Do you know what happened when I tried to get in a few rides at the arena yesterday? Kaylie Johnson showed up. And Betty Rainey. And Shannon Frazier. And that's not even the worst of it. Shannon brought a peach cobbler. And you know how much I love peach cobbler."

"Don't tell me you ate it."

"No, but I came damn close. Luckily Eli was going to see his sweetie for a date and so I passed it off to him just to get it out of my sight. Otherwise, I would have eaten the whole damned thing and given that poor girl a lot of false hope. This way I won't be eating anybody's peach cobbler."

"And what about Nikki? What about her cobbler?"

He thought of Nikki's comments about the food

at the wedding. "She doesn't do cobblers, so I think I'm good."

"I wouldn't be too sure about that. Every woman has a good cobbler in her. If the right man comes along."

But Cole wasn't the right man. Not even close. Which was why she'd managed to put on the brakes when he'd been ready to go balls to the wall in the sack.

No, she had other things on her mind at this point in her life, and so she was in no hurry to complicate their arrangement.

That's what he told himself, but damned if he believed it. Something else was holding her back. He just didn't know what it was. Not that he was going to waste brain power trying to figure it out.

This wasn't about sex.

"I know this is a little hard to understand, but Nikki and I are helping each other out, at least until I roll out of town. Then we'll make a public split and it'll all be over. Listen, bro, keep it quiet, okay?"

"You can trust me."

But Cole already knew that. There were only a handful of people that he could put his faith in and Jesse was at the top of the list. And Billy. And Pete. Beyond that, Cole didn't place any bets.

"So where's the money?" he asked, eager to change the subject.

Jesse went quiet and Cole started to worry that his oldest brother wasn't going to let the subject drop. But finally his voice carried over the line. "Still out at Big Earl's place. I didn't have a chance to stash it at my place before the ceremony, and then it was late when we finished up. Casey is dropping it by in the morning."

"And expecting a cut."

"She knows she's not getting a penny of this money. I'm paying her out of my own pocket for keeping her mouth shut and helping us."

"I'll pay half."

"Don't even think about it. I know you're only agreeing to all of this because of me."

"I just don't see that it's going to change anything. We are who we are."

"It might change how people see us."

But other people's opinions weren't Cole's problem. He knew who he was. What he was. *That* was the real problem.

Before he could dwell on the sobering thought, Jesse's voice drew his attention. "Since you're stuck here, we need to make the most of it. We don't have too many good broncs on hand at the training facility, but I know where I can get a few to tide you over. That is, if you manage to drag your lazy ass out of Nikki Barbie's bed."

"More like off her couch." When he finally managed to settle down, that is. As it was, he needed to move, to breathe in some fresh air and get his body back in check.

"Trouble in paradise already?"

"Something like that."

Jesse's voice grew quiet for a long moment before he said, "I hope you know what you're doing."

"So do I." Cole fought down a wave of misgivings and the crazy urge to waltz into the kitchen just to see what Nikki had cooking. It didn't matter how good it smelled, he wasn't interested. He didn't do that froufrou crap. He liked good old-fashioned home cooking. Something substantial. Like meat and potatoes and cobbler. Lots of cobbler.

"Listen," he went on, eager to kill the thought, "call Casey and tell her I'm picking up the money tonight. There's no sense in waiting until morning when I've got some time on my hands right now." Cole hung up the phone and listened to Nikki move around in the kitchen. The delicious aroma that drifted down the hallway grew more intense. More enticing. His nostrils flared as he climbed out of bed.

He slipped on his shirt and jeans, and barely resisted the urge to head for the kitchen. As hungry as he was, for her and the food, he wasn't about to pursue either. His "marriage" was all about eliminating the distractions.

And that's what he intended to do by getting the

hell out of here before he did something crazy like waltz into the kitchen, lift her up onto the nearest counter and slide fast, sure and deep inside her warm body.

He stiffened against the notion, pulled on his boots, grabbed his keys and headed for the door.

6

HE WAS GONE.

The truth echoed in Nikki's head as the door slammed shut and the walls of the kitchen rattled. A rush of disappointment went through her.

Hello? It's not like he's going to stick around for pancakes and eggs.

Sure, they were married but in theory only. There would be no hot, frantic sex, no late-night cuddling afterward, no mornings spent chatting over the breakfast table.

He would do his thing and she would do hers.

Which, at the moment, was a technically difficult sauce that seemed to be kicking her butt.

She needed more butter. And some heavy cream. And just a hint of parsley.

Seriously, it's not like she'd expected him to duck in and say goodbye. He didn't have to document every time he went out in the middle of the friggin' night just because they'd said "I do."

Sure, she was his wife. But she wasn't his *wife*.

She fought down another sliver of disappointment and adjusted the fire on the burner. Time to perfect her sauce. And then maybe try her hand at a crepe. But not just any crepe. One loaded with strawberries and fresh cream and a berry reduction.

Not too sweet, but plenty sweet enough to sate the sudden hunger that twisted at her insides.

Once upon a time, maybe.

But thinking about strawberries and cream when all she really wanted was a piece of her late grandmother's decadent chocolate cake made her stomach grumble that much more.

Her attention went to a nearby cabinet and the recipe box she knew was stashed inside. A few feet, a quick reach and she would be on her way to a nice, big, rich piece of chocolate goodness. But it was late and she really was busy.

Too busy doing what she knew she should do instead of what she wanted to.

"You're different, Nikki girl. You ain't like your momma and your sisters. You got heart. Drive. You're the sweetest child in this whole world and it'll take you far. Don't give up on your dreams just 'cause somebody tells you to."

A sweet child with a sweet tooth thanks to her

grandmother Ruth who'd whipped up the richest, most decadent desserts in town and sold them to the local eating establishments. Nikki had licked the bowl one too many times to count when Ruth had been busy working on a particular order for the local diner or the weekly Lion's Club luncheon.

Recipes she'd once made for her husband who'd never appreciated them near as much as any paying customer. He'd left her despite her way around the kitchen and she'd been stuck raising Raylene on her own.

She'd done her best, using her decadent desserts to make ends meet, but times had still been rough. Not only financially, but emotionally. The break-up had happened when Raylene had been young and impressionable, and Nikki's mother had never been able to forgive the father who'd deserted her. She'd grown up with a serious distrust of men, and a determination to make it without one.

And she'd raised her daughters to do the same.

She didn't want them to be mild and meek like her own mother. The type of woman who caught her man cheating and, instead of kicking him out, baked him his favorite dessert to bribe him to stay.

A homemade chocolate cake with Dr. Pepper frosting.

Nikki's favorite.

Not that her mother knew as much. Grammy Ruth

had given her the recipe box when she'd been just six. For safekeeping, the woman had said just weeks before she'd had a massive heart attack, as if she'd known her days were numbered.

Nikki had stashed the box in the back of her closet, but she'd never forgotten it. She'd thought of the recipes too many times to count, but she'd never actually made anything.

Because of her mother.

Raylene would have freaked if she'd caught Nikki making one of Ruth's recipes, and so she'd left the recipe box alone to keep the peace with her mother.

She certainly hadn't ignored it all these years because it brought back too many happy memories. Of a better time when she hadn't felt so isolated. So different.

Because her grammy had accepted her for who'd she'd been, and loved her anyway. And remembering only made going through the motions now that much more difficult.

She ditched the thought and focused her attention on unwrapping two sticks of butter.

Besides, a Dr. Pepper cake wasn't going to land her an internship at a Michelin-starred restaurant. She needed real food for that. Sophisticated, refined offerings that wowed the palate and taste buds.

Which was why she'd altered her eating habits way back when and started stopping off for lunch at various restaurants in Austin whenever she picked up supplies for the honky-tonk. She'd experimented with food, tasting everything from duck confit to foie gras. And she'd even learned to like most of it. To the point that her mouth no longer watered for the decadent cake.

Most of the time.

Her stomach hollowed out and she reached for the butter. Her hands trembled as she unwrapped yet another stick and fought the urge to haul down the recipe box. Not no, but *hell* no. She'd sampled enough of the forbidden for one night.

Time to toss the half-eaten fruit, get the hell out of Eden and walk the straight and narrow directly to her dream job. Her finals and then Houston.

She'd already applied for three positions, the first of which she should be hearing back on in just a matter of days.

All the more reason to buckle down and focus. And forget.

The Dr. Pepper frosting *and* Cole Chisholm.

FORGETTING WAS DAMNED hard to do when she kept being reminded of what a hunk she'd married last night.

How good-looking.

How sexy.

How decadent.

Nikki peeked past the door of her bedroom to see him stretched out on her couch.

He'd not only come back last night, but he'd peeled off everything but his jeans and was now flat on his back, half-naked right in front of her. His chest rose and fell with the steady rhythm of his breathing and her gaze riveted on the silky brown hair that ran from nipple to nipple before narrowing to a delicious vee that disappeared into the waistband of his low-slung denim.

A shadow covered his jaw and his hair was mussed as if he hadn't slept any more soundly than she had.

He hadn't.

She'd heard the door just a few minutes after she'd finally called it a night, the squeak of springs as he'd settled on her sofa, the thud of boots as he'd tossed them nearby, her own disappointed sigh because he hadn't so much as knocked on her door.

While she wasn't about to partake of the forbidden fruit, it would at least be nice to have it offered.

But after three sleepless hours, she knew that wasn't going to happen. Obviously Cole had had time to think about what had happened and he'd come to the conclusion that the idea of them falling into bed was bad with a capital *B,* just as she'd said.

When the sun had topped the horizon, she'd given up the attempt at sleep. She'd dragged herself up and doused herself with a cold shower before pulling on her usual work uniform—blue-jean shorts, a skimpy tank top with *Giddyup* written in neon pink and cowboy boots. The bar was closed today, but that didn't mean there was any less to do. Sundays were spent restocking and cleaning and prepping for Manic Monday and the all-you-can-eat rib buffet that Raylene offered during happy hour to bring in the customers.

Her sisters usually handled the bar area while Nikki spent her time in the kitchen, but since they were in Hawaii for their honeymoon, that meant three times the workload.

Unless her mother showed up.

She would. Eventually. Nikki had no doubt about that.

She'd been in shock last night and so she'd kept her distance. But eventually she would get mad and determined to give her youngest a great big piece of her mind. And a huge guilt trip.

Nikki would have to face both, but hopefully not just yet. Not after last night's encounter and so little sleep and a lumpy béarnaise sauce. She was already having one heck of a bad day.

She sent up a silent prayer that Raylene would spend the day nursing a massive hangover courtesy of the tequila she'd consumed last night while mourning the loss of yet another daughter to one Cole Chisholm.

Speaking of which…

She tiptoed past him, past the shirt tossed on the floor and the boot lying on its side and a large black duffel bag, and tried to breathe. Fat chance when he shifted and she stalled.

She fought to ignore the ripple of his bicep as he stuffed a hand under his head and forced herself to breathe as he settled back down. Another step and she reached for her purse which sat on the coffee table next to his cowboy hat.

A few frantic heartbeats later, she headed down the steps that ran behind the bar. Digging for her keys, she started to open the door only to find it unlocked.

So much for escaping a confrontation right now.

Dread washed through and her heart stalled because there was no doubt in her mind, Raylene was inside and the shit was about to hit the fan.

7

"MA! I KNOW YOU'RE in there," she called out as she walked inside, "and I just want to say… Wow, your beard looks really long."

"You like?" asked the young man who met her a few feet inside the doorway. He stroked the thick, bushy length of brown hair hanging from his narrow chin. "It's my new *Duck Dynasty* look. It's not real. Just a fake one I picked up at the Rite Aid—part of the leftover costumes from Halloween—but you get the idea. This is how I'm going to grow it out."

Just as soon as the testosterone kicked in, which wasn't likely to be in the near future since Colby Jackson was already twenty-three, and still only five foot two and one hundred and forty pounds wet. He normally had zero facial hair except for the occasional lone whisker that sprouted on his otherwise baby-soft face. He had blue eyes, a sweet smile and a strong work ethic, which was why Raylene had hired him to wash glasses and sweep floors. He came in early and stayed late and never complained.

At least not in front of Raylene.

"We should have a *Duck Dynasty* night instead of Women's Wednesday," he went on. "We could install some giant flat-screen TVs over the bar and put up some camo decorations. Everybody would show up here to watch the show and drink a Si Tai."

"A Si Tai?"

"You know. A drink named after Silas, the *Duck Dynasty* uncle. I bet every man in town would like that."

"Maybe, but they like meeting women even more and so we do Women's Wednesdays so the ladies get in free and the men pay because they want to get in and meet some ladies."

"I think *Duck Dynasty* is a better idea."

"You would."

"What's that supposed to mean?"

"That you have no social life." When he gave her a sharp look, she added, "Don't worry. Your secret is safe with me." Namely because Colby was one of the few people who actually knew that Nikki didn't live up to her look. He'd saved her on more than one occasion from an overly flirty guy by calling her back into the kitchen to check the wings, or dish up some pretzels. Colby was her friend.

"Thank heavens it's you." She followed him into the main area where the dance floor sat flanked by three massive bars. "I thought Mom was here."

"Haven't seen her and I've been here going on two hours. Mopped all the floors and I'm about to start cleaning the bathrooms, though I don't expect there'll be much of a mess since I cleaned on Friday night and we were closed yesterday for the wedding." A sadness touched his eyes, along with a gleam of awe. "I bet April looked awful pretty."

"You should have come to see for yourself. You were invited."

"And see that Jake Barber fawning all over her?" He puffed out his chest. "No thanks."

"Jake is a nice guy. He'll be good to her."

"I could have been good to her." He seemed deflated and suddenly the whole *Duck Dynasty* beard made sense. He was feeling inadequate because his crush had chosen someone else.

She knew the feeling.

Way back when, Cole Chisholm had been her crush.

She'd watched him chase after everything in a skirt all through middle school and high school, when all she'd ever wanted was for him to chase after her.

Fat chance.

He'd been six years older than her and so he'd never seen her as anything other than a kid.

Still…she'd wanted him to at least notice her. Even just a little.

Much the way Colby had hoped for April to finally notice him.

She hadn't, any more than Cole had paid Nikki no nevermind.

And now you're married to the guy.

But it wasn't real. Even if it had felt just that for a split second last night when she'd been in his arms and he'd been kissing her and—

"We should get to work." She walked behind the bar and reached for an apron stashed just to the left of the cash register. "The sooner we start, the sooner we can wrap it up."

"Yeah." He turned toward the bucket and mop. "But just so you know, I won't be doing this forever. I've got plans. Ideas. I'm going to hit it big one day and I'll be a hundred times better than some stupid steer wrestler. And then she'll be sorry."

"I'm sure she will be." Her gaze met the young man's and she gave him a sympathetic smile. "Don't worry about her, Colby. You'll make some girl very happy someday and you'll forget all about April." He nodded, but she knew he wasn't the least bit convinced.

She didn't blame him.

She'd told herself to forget Cole all those years ago, and still he'd lived on in her fantasies.

Which made what should have been a simple fake marriage of convenience much more complicated than her inebriated brain had anticipated last night.

Not that she was changing her mind and backing out now. Her Sundays were usually spent doing inventory and cleaning toilets and restocking the bar—under her mother's watchful eye, that was. But Raylene had yet to even show up, and so Nikki went on to spend the day in the honky-tonk's sizable kitchen, working on more béarnaise sauce and even a steak tartare. She perfected both, too, thanks to nine hours of uninterrupted concentration.

It turned into the most productive day she'd had in...well, forever, and a taste of what it would be like to spend her days doing only what she loved. No slinging hash at the bar, no avoiding her mother, no pretending to be something she wasn't. Just hours and hours filled with her passion. Her purpose.

She sampled the tartare.

Okay, so maybe she wasn't that passionate about the complicated dish. While tasty, it just wasn't nearly as filling as it should have been.

Earth to Nikki? It's an appetizer. It's not supposed to fill you up. Just whet the appetite. Zing the taste buds. And pave the way for the real star of the meal— the entrée.

She took another bite and ignored the sudden crav-

ing for a cold slice of pizza sitting in the nearby refrigerator.

No pizza. No fast food. Nothing that kills the palate.

She settled for a third bite and a long swig of water
before turning to work on the massive pile of dishes
created by one small plate of near-raw beef.

A half hour later, she locked up the bar and headed
around to the back staircase. A single bulb buzzed
overhead surrounded by a flurry of tiny moths. The
rear parking lot sat empty except for her ancient
Chevy single cab parked near the stairs and a small
Dumpster that sat at the side of the building.

Which meant that Cole Chisholm wasn't still
asleep on her couch.

Not that she'd expected as much.

It was nine hours since she'd left the apartment
and the man did have a life. It wasn't like he was
going to sit around waiting for her to come home so
they could play house. He was probably at the arena,
giving some bronc hell.

Thankfully.

She'd had an incredibly productive day for the first
time in a long time, and fighting with her own raging hormones would definitely kill her good mood.
As it was, she wanted a shower and a good night's
sleep, and she wanted both without worrying if Cole
Chisholm was stretched out half-naked on her sofa.

While she had no doubt he would come back eventually—he'd brought a monstrous duffel bag, after all—she desperately hoped it wouldn't be until much later. Long after she'd climbed into bed and fallen fast asleep.

Just give me a few hours. She sent up the silent prayer and mounted the steps.

At the top, she crossed the small concrete walkway and reached for the doorknob.

It swung inward before she could so much as close her fingers around the metal, and she realized in a startling instant that like most men, the big guy upstairs hadn't heard a word she'd said.

Because Nikki Barbie wasn't alone.

8

COLE WAS HOME.

That's what she told herself as she walked into the dark interior of her apartment and saw the shadow sitting on the sofa. Waiting.

Cole had ditched his car and walked, and he was here now. Home to the little wifey.

The shadow shifted and fear raced up her spine because no way was that Cole. The shoulders were too narrow. The physique too thin.

It was someone else.

A burglar ransacking the place and stealing her blind? A mass murderer who'd decided to carve her up like a Thanksgiving turkey and make her his next victim? She debated between the two as anxiety rolled through her, followed by a rush of dread when she caught the familiar scent of perfume and Marlboro cigarettes.

Forget the burglar or the mass murderer. It was worse, much worse.

"I thought about getting married once." Raylene's familiar voice bounced off the walls and the anxiety turned to full-blown fear.

It was worse, all right.

It was her mother.

"I was staying with my grandmother down in Port Aransas for a summer," her voice echoed in the shadowy room. "You never knew her. She died before you and your sisters were born. She was a decent woman. Needy like my mother, but then that was the way with most women back then. My grandfather died early on, so I never really knew him. Just her. She didn't cook much. We did mostly sandwiches when I went to stay with her. She had this little place on the beach. A small house, but I always thought that it would make one hell of a bar. A little place to dish up margaritas and listen to music. Of course, it's little more than a run-down shack now, but with a little work..." Her voice trailed off and faded into the frantic beat of Nikki's own heart.

"Mom, are you okay?"

"No," she bit out. "I'm not okay. Not at all." Her words were cool and precise, just like Raylene most of the time. But there was an undercurrent moving through the room, like a storm brewing, waiting for the first lightning strike.

"That's where I got the initial idea for the Gid-dyup," Raylene went on. "Of course, it's a lot bigger than any tiny beach bar, but then I wanted something substantial for you girls. Something you could call your own so you would never have to worry about money." A bitter laugh followed. "Fat chance of that. I can barely pay salaries as it is."

The comment caught her off guard and Nikki couldn't help herself. She'd meant to let her mother get it all out, and get the confrontation over with, but the words were out before she could stop them. "I thought the bar was doing good."

"Good for a small town. That means I can make the payments on three different mortgages, but a profit? In my dreams. No, I'm just making ends meet. But there won't be much chance of that now with everyone gone. I'll have to hire some people and I can barely afford what I have."

"I didn't know—"

"Don't interrupt the story," she cut in, her voice pinched and Nikki knew immediately while she wasn't drunk, she'd had a few drinks.

"Why don't you let me make some coffee and then you can tell the story—"

"No," she cut in. "I'm telling my story and you're going to listen. I was seventeen and he was nineteen and, well, it was the best sex I'd had in a long time and that can mess up a woman's thinking. I thought about it, but then I caught him kissing another girl. I wasn't even mad. No, I was grateful because he'd done me a huge favor by showing his true colors before I made a big mistake. That's what's going to happen to you." She pushed to her feet. "He's going to cheat and you're going to be humiliated and then you're going to come running back here. But there won't be a here."

"What's that supposed to mean?"

"No sense in me busting my ass every day to give you something so that you don't need a man, when you up and marry one anyway. Not when I could be lazing on the beach with a margarita." She pushed to her feet and started pacing. "Twenty-seven years I sacrificed," Raylene moaned. "Twenty-seven years busting my ass, trying to raise you girls, to teach you something, and for what? So you could go off and chain yourself to a bunch of rodeo heathens. I raised you better than this."

I'm sorry. It's not real. Don't hate me.

The words jumped to the tip of her tongue, but she fought them back down and gathered her courage. "I didn't mean for it to happen."

"Then put a stop to it now." Raylene turned on her. The dim glow of the kitchen light nearby pushed into the room, casting a slither of light across her desperate face. "Kick him out and we'll chalk it up to nerves and we'll go downstairs right now and I'll show you how to make a Bloody Mary with a twist." Crazed hope lit her eyes. "I can show you how to make anything you want and then you can handle the bar while I run the floor. It'll be just the two of us. Forever."

"We fell for each other," Nikki blurted, the prospect of spending the rest of her life at the Giddyup sparking a rush of raw anxiety. "It was love at first sight."

"It was lust." Raylene shrugged. "You're horny. I understand. A woman has needs."

That she should never, ever discuss with her own mother.

"It's not like that."

"Sure, it is. He's good-looking. I'm sure he has a great big—"

"We're in love." The words tumbled out of Nikki's mouth so fast that they almost tripped over one another. "I love him and he loves me." She didn't mean to say it. She was already near smoking from all the lies, but then Raylene wanted to talk about Cole's you-know-what and it was a conversation she wasn't ready to have with herself, much less her mother. "We're soul mates."

"No." Raylene shook her head frantically. "Don't say such a thing."

"We might even get matching shirts—"

"Stop!" Raylene's face turned red and then purple, but she didn't say anything. She just stood there, as if trying to decide whether to strangle Nikki or throw herself out the nearest window. "I see," she finally said, her voice quiet. "I guess there's nothing else to say." She snatched up her purse and pushed past Nikki. "I need to get out of here. You'll regret this," she muttered, marching past Nikki. "Mark my words." And then she did what Nikki had been waiting for since the idea had sparked last night—she marched through the door without another word. Hinges creaked and wood cracked and the door slammed, and it was done.

Nikki fought down her guilt and the urge to go after her.

If she did that, she could kiss goodbye her dream of ever being a professional chef. No acing her finals. No internship. No five-star restaurant.

Nothing but fried pickles and Bloody Marys and Raylene for the rest of her life.

While she loved her mother, she didn't want to spend a lifetime with her.

No, she was doing the right thing. The only thing. Her back was to the wall and a fake marriage with Cole Chisholm was the only way out.

He'd reached out a hand to her. Her savior. Her hero.

Again.

The notion stirred a familiar rush of heat and she found herself wondering when he would come back.

And whether or not he would pull off his shirt and stretch out on her couch and—

Her stomach grumbled and she knew she didn't stand a chance in hell of relaxing or falling asleep right now.

Which meant there was no better time than the present to get started on her next dish for finals.

She drew a deep breath and tried to calm her frantic heartbeat. She'd done it. She'd faced off with her mother and now there would be blessed distance. Two weeks of it and then it was *Houston, here I come.*

The worst was over.

She held tight to the knowledge as she headed for the kitchen.

OKAY, SO MAYBE the worst was just getting started.

Nikki came to that realization several hours later as she tossed and turned and tried to forget the all-important fact that Cole was back. And on her sofa. And half-naked.

He'd come in a few hours ago and she'd retreated into her room, and she'd been fighting the urge to take a peek ever since.

Maybe he kept his shirt on.

That's what she told herself. But men like Cole Chisholm didn't sleep with their shirts on. They took them off. And maybe even their pants. And their undies.

If they even wore undies.

Ugh. Raylene had been right. Nikki was horny.

She stifled the thought and tried to shut her eyes, but the question kept haunting her—briefs or commando?—until she finally threw back the covers and tiptoed to the door.

Just a quick peek and then her curiosity would be satisfied. He would still have his jeans on like last night and she could forget all about her crazy speculation.

Her hand was just shy of the doorknob when she heard Cole's deep voice on the other side.

"Nikki?" A knock followed. "It's Cole. We need to talk."

Okay, so maybe he wanted to give her a first-hand look.

Her heart kicked up a notch only to take a nose-dive south when she opened the door to see the murderous look on his face.

"What's wrong?"

"It's gone," he declared. He shook his head as if he couldn't quite believe it. "Gone. It was here earlier, but when I went to grab it, nothing."

"What's gone?"

"The money. My money."

"But your wallet's on the coffee table."

"Not the money in my wallet. The *money*. The hundred thousand dollars my father stole from that bank. I had it right here in a black duffel bag and now it's gone."

Her mind rifled back and she remembered the black duffel. It had been there earlier and then…

An image stirred. Of Raylene snagging her purse, or what Nikki thought had been her purse, and marching past, out the door. *Gone.*

"I had it right here and now it's gone," Cole went on, his voice low and deadly a split second before his accusing stare landed on her. "And I damn well want it back."

9

"ARE YOU OKAY?" Cole asked the next morning as he followed Nikki onto a monstrous RV-like black bus that had his name and sponsor list blazing in full neon green on the side. The bus, along with others like it dedicated to various rodeo stars and several livestock trailers, was parked in a lot near the Lost Gun Rodeo Arena.

"I'm fine." Nikki stalled on the top step and stared at the interior. "Excited, even. All brides are excited on their honeymoon. Don't I look excited?"

"No, you look nervous." He came up directly behind her, dwarfing her with his large frame. "But then wild and wicked Nikki Barbie doesn't get nervous, right?"

"Not at all." She should be used to his nearness by now, especially after being cooped up in a pickup truck with him for several hours for the past couple of days. But he'd been busy driving at the time and so she hadn't had to worry about drawing his full attention.

But this… Her gaze shifted in time to see him close the door behind them. This was just the two of them. Alone. Together. With no place to escape to should her hormones start raging.

She dropped her bag to the side and stepped forward to survey the interior and put some distance between them. She bypassed a small eating area that consisted of a booth-like table on one side and refrigerator, convection oven and stove on the other. Next came a small living area with two plush leather recliners on one side and a massive flat-screen TV on the other. A few more steps and she reached a sleeping space with a full-size bed on one side and a large closet on the other. Two more steps and the aisle dead-ended into a second bed.

"You're definitely nervous." Cole's voice sounded directly behind her and she stiffened.

"Well, I'm not, and if you start with the whole 'Are you afraid to ride on a bus?' thing, I'm going to slip rat poisoning into your peanut-butter-and-jelly sandwich." She turned and ducked under his arm to put a few blessed footsteps between them again.

"I didn't think you were afraid of riding on a bus. We're not going to ride in it. We're going to sleep in it."

"Well, I'm not afraid of that, either." *Yeah, right.*

It was one thing to have a nice solid wall between them and a small portion of hallway and an actual door, and quite another to be less than a few feet away, and in full view.

She opened the one doorway that sat between the beds and eyed the small shower just tall enough to accommodate Cole. A small toilet sat nearby.

"There's not much room in here, is there?"

"It's actually one of the biggest buses on the circuit. I bought it last year when I won the finals. It makes getting to and from events a helluva lot easier. A driver can drive while I sleep."

Nikki's mind rushed back to the moment she'd caught sight of Cole's bus back in Lost Gun. It *had* looked large at first glance. But standing smack-dab inside with Cole so close, she marveled at how anyone could actually breathe in one of these things. Despite the sizable skylight built into the main compartment's ceiling.

"My driver usually bunks out in here with me, or Eli, but since he and Melba are an item now, I'll be flying solo on this trip. We'll have the bus all to ourselves."

"I still don't understand why we just can't take my car and get a couple of motel rooms along the way—"

"Seriously?" he cut in. "This place is a hundred times better than any motel room."

She eyed the plush interior. She certainly couldn't argue with that.

"I just hate to put you out—"

"Man, you really *are* nervous."

"Like hell." She closed the bathroom door and checked out the small television and stereo built into the wall at the foot of the first bed. She punched a few buttons on the remote and the stereo lit up. A classic country song burst from the speakers.

"Eli's a Johnny Cash fanatic." Cole came up and pressed the button. The stereo fell silent.

"I had him pegged more for a Hank Williams Jr. fan." She inched to the side, away from him.

"I wouldn't say that to his face. You're liable to start a war. He considers Johnny the king." He headed up the aisle toward the kitchen area. "Can I get you something to drink?"

"I'm good."

"Suit yourself." He shrugged and retrieved a Gatorade. Twisting off the cap, he took a long drink and Nikki tried to ignore the picture he made standing there, head thrown back, guzzling the icy liquid.

Are you deaf? a voice whispered. *I said "ignore." That means not noticing the way his throat muscles worked, or the way that single drop of liquid slid down his tanned skin, or the way his muscles flexed as he tightened his hand around the bottle.*

She tore her gaze away and folded down the cov-

ers on her bed before she had to face the next challenge—retrieving her overnight bag from near the
front doorway. The walkway accommodated one person, no problem.

But two?

Maybe.

If she plastered herself against the far side and
eased past just so, she might avoid any actual contact.

Dream on.

He stepped to the side, but there simply wasn't
enough room. One hard, sinewy shoulder brushed
hers and his muscled bicep touched the side of her
breast. Her breath caught and her heart jumped.

Strong fingers closed around her upper arm and
he stared down at her.

Okay, so accidental touching was bad enough, but
the fingers on her arm were there on purpose. Strong.
Sure. Stirring.

Uh-oh.

"Hey, are you really okay?"

"Fine," she blurted, expelling the breath. "I'm just
thinking about my mom. And my finals."

The floor seemed to tilt and it got really hot, really fast.

Just breathe. In and out. In and out.

His gaze narrowed as he studied her. "Are you
hyperventilating?"

"I am not." Was she? Oh, hell, she was.

She tried to slow her sudden breathing. Impossible considering the fact that he was still touching her arm. His fingers burned into her flesh, sending a rush of heat to every major erogenous zone.

"You sure as hell are. You're hyperventilating."

"I am *not*..." The last word didn't come out with near enough emphasis considering she couldn't quite catch her breath.

His gaze narrowed. "Are you claustrophobic?"

"Of course not." Okay, so why had she said that? She should have screamed a big fat yes, made a beeline for the door and spent the rest of the night in a nearby hotel.

An easy solution for a big problem.

Except that she knew Cole would never let her go alone. He didn't trust her. That meant keeping an eye on her twenty-four seven and so he would surely follow. And then they would register for one room because no way could they register for separate rooms. The press was crawling all over the area thanks to tomorrow's rodeo and so someone would surely see them. They could kiss goodbye all the headlines they'd made as rodeo's newly married sweethearts.

She eyed the granite countertops and the stainless-steel stove and an idea struck. At least in the RV she could actually keep herself busy doing what she loved to do.

"I'm hungry," she blurted. "I didn't eat nearly

enough for lunch. Once I get something in my stomach, I'm sure I'll feel much better." She forced a slow, deep breath and clung to the one and only bright side of sleeping on the bus—at least they had separate beds.

Separate, she told herself for the rest of the night. And she might have believed it if it didn't feel as if they were practically in the same room. Above the hum of the air conditioner, she could actually hear his soft snores. The brush of skin against cotton as he rolled one way and then the other.

She did some rolling of her own, tossing this way and that, mentally going over the last conversation with her mother in a desperate attempt to distract herself and figure out some clue as to where the woman was headed.

If she was actually heading anywhere. She might just be on the run, going as fast and as far as possible.

Maybe.

She was close by. She hadn't purchased an airline ticket or taken a bus. Even more, she'd stopped at the rest area not ten miles outside of town. And she'd charged dinner at the local diner. She'd either been here recently, or she was still here.

Close.

Not nearly as close as Cole.

Her ears perked and the sound of his deep even breaths echoed and her nipples pebbled.

Ugh. It was going to be a long, *long* night.

"So you're sure you didn't see this woman in here yesterday?" Cole flashed the picture to the clerk behind the counter at the Waller General Store.

The young woman—maybe eighteen or nineteen with a brown ponytail and a disinterested expression—shrugged. "Maybe."

"Her credit card was swiped here at three-thirty in the afternoon." He knew because he and Nikki had logged on and checked the credit card transactions online just a few hours ago to see what had posted. "A transaction in the amount of seventeen dollars and sixty-two cents. At exactly 3:32 p.m. That's what showed up in the online transactions."

"Then I guess so. Say—" her gaze narrowed "—don't I know you?"

"I don't think so."

"I do. I know I do." She eyed him again. "Mr. Walker?" She motioned to the old man standing near the hardware section. He looked to be in his seventies, with a red gingham shirt tucked into stiff Wranglers.

"What can I do you for, Miss Jamie?"

"This here fella looks familiar. Don't you think?"

The man eyed him and it was as if a lightbulb went on in his head. "Why, you're that saddle-bronc rider, aren't you? That there rodeo star?"

"Cole Chisholm." Cole held out his hand to the

man who looked at it like it was a great big diamond-back about to strike.

"Cole Chisholm? *The* Cole Chisholm?"

"Last time I looked at my birth certificate."

"Well, I'll be a monkey's uncle." The man let loose a low whistle and slid his hand into Cole's for a vigorous shake. "What the heck are you doin' in Waller?"

"Just passing through."

"On your way to Vegas? 'Cause you're way off if that's the case."

"A road trip," he blurted. His gaze went to the fast-growing group of people surrounding them and the cluster of young women just to his left. High-school age and much too young, but still. "My new wife and I are cruising around, seeing the sights before I head for the finals. Sort of an unofficial honeymoon."

"Well, I'll be." The man whistled again. "Say, we've got our annual pickle festival goin' on down at the fairgrounds right now. Why don't you stop on by and let us show you a little hospitality." When Cole opened his mouth to refuse, the man added, "I know the kids would love it. Got some mutton bustin' happenin' at the same time as the pickle competition. I know that ain't exactly your area of expertise, but I know the boys would be tickled pink to meet you and have you give 'em a little pep talk afore the event."

"I don't..." he started, but the man looked so hopeful. And while Cole might not be much for all the hurrah and PR stuff that went with being a five-time buckle winner, he did everything he could when it came to kids. From donating a scholarship to the local 4-H club, to making a special appearance for the Make-A-Wish Foundation just last year when he'd visited a little boy named Keith. He thought of the smile on the eight-year-old's face and the awful smell of red carnations six months later.

"I'll be there." Besides, it wasn't as if he had any intense detective work to do. Raylene had swiped her card at the general store yesterday, but since then, nothing. Which meant she'd probably moved on. While he meant to keep asking around for the next hour or so, after that there was really nothing to do but wait until she made another move and follow the trail.

Until then…

"I'd be happy to help out with the kids," he told the old man.

"Great. That's just great. Say, you could even come on over to the pickle competition afterward and try all the goodies. Make it a whole evenin' of fun." The man took Cole's hand again and shook it profusely before Cole managed to disengage. A low whistle followed as he turned away, along with a chuckle and a "Why, I'll be a monkey's uncle *and* his aunt. *The* Cole Chisholm…"

10

Nikki stared at the cluster of flowers waiting for her when she walked into the RV. The rich, fragrant aroma tickled her nostrils as her gaze shifted to Cole. "A token from one of your many admirers?"

"Something like that."

"I never figured you for the flower sort."

"They're not for me. They're for you. I was in town and some guys at the general store recognized me. They insisted I bring these to you." He handed her the card which read *Congratulations on Getting Hitched*.

"They're having their annual pickle festival down at the rodeo grounds. They asked if we would come as their special guests."

"Are you going?"

"Not me, sugar. Us." He pulled a small box out of his pocket and handed it to her. "We're married now."

Her heart paused as she took the small velvet square and her stomach hollowed out. "This isn't what I think it is."

"You can't be married without a ring." He held up his hand and she noted the small, simple gold band. "Go ahead. Open it."

She lifted the lid and stared at the solitaire-cut diamond ring surrounded by rubies and a lump jumped into her throat.

A crazy reaction because she knew it wasn't real. This wasn't real.

"Do you like it?" If she hadn't known better, she would have sworn she heard a thread of hope in his voice.

As if her opinion mattered.

As if.

She forced a deep breath and tried to calm her racing heart. "I, um…" Where the hell was her voice when she really needed it? "That is, I, um, think it'll do just fine. It's nice. For a fake." It had to be a fake. Because no man would give a woman such a nice ring—a beautiful ring—just for pretend.

The realization sent a tingle of disappointment through her, followed by a rush of heat when he took the piece of jewelry from the box.

Time seemed to stand still in that next instant as his strong fingers touched hers. Skin met skin.

Electricity rushed from the point of contact, zapping every nerve as he slid the ring onto her finger.

"There." His gaze met hers. "Now we won't have to worry about stirring any suspicion."

And there it was. The real reason he'd gone to so much trouble.

She stifled a pang of hurt and tried for a laugh. "Talk about a heartfelt proposal. You should write greeting cards."

"This isn't a proposal, sugar. We're already married." He stared at her, as if trying to see what simmered below the surface. "I never figured you for the romantic type," he said after a long moment. There was a teasing note in his voice, but it didn't quite touch his gaze.

She shrugged. "Yeah, well, I guess the roses are putting me in the mood." She tried for another smile, eager to cover her temporary slip. "You'd better watch out. Next, I'll be expecting a box of chocolates."

"Maybe later." He grinned. "But for now you'll have to settle for a jar of pickles." He motioned to the row sitting on a nearby counter. "Courtesy of the Hanover County Pickle Committee."

She remembered the welcome sign at the entrance to the small town. "Wedding present?"

"More like a bribe. They want us to judge the pickle-eating contest." The grin faded and his lips drew into a serious expression. "Listen, I'm sorry I got so pissed yesterday. I know this isn't your fault. You couldn't have known your mother would do something like this and then take off."

But she knew where she was going.

She stifled the thought. While she had her suspicions, she didn't know for sure. She wasn't going to tell Cole about her hunch, only to have Raylene turn tail and head for Colorado or Arizona or any number of places and prove her wrong. It was still too early to tell.

On top of that, we were talking her *mother.*

While she and Raylene didn't see eye to eye, she didn't want to see her mother face any theft charges. Better to catch up to the woman first and recover the money. Raylene could make a getaway while Nikki handed the money back over to Cole.

And if she'd already spent it?

Doubtful. She wanted to fix up the place in Port Aransas, which meant she would need every penny. Which explained why she was using the credit card along the way rather than forking over her cash.

Still, if she had spent some of the heist money, Nikki would have to find some way to get it back.

She thought of the stash she'd been saving for the past three years for living expenses to tide her over in Houston. Her dream money.

And if she'd managed somehow, someway to spend all of it?

She forced aside the disastrous thought. She'd seen the look in her mother's eyes when she'd talked about Port Aransas. The place was important to her. Enough that she'd swiped one hundred thousand dollars to restore it. She wouldn't spend it before she got there.

Which meant Nikki still had time. It was just a matter of getting to Raylene before Cole did.

But first she had a pickle-eating contest to judge.

"What?" he asked, obviously noting her worried expression. "Don't tell me you're allergic to pickles."

"No, I'm just not up for eating about a zillion of them." She forced a smile. "But duty calls, right?"

"Atta girl." He held out a hand. "Just pace yourself. You'll be fine."

Warning bells sounded in Nikki's head as she stared up into Cole's deep violet eyes. She should say no. Make some excuse about following up a lead while he went about with his PR stuff. Stay as far away as possible from him.

She would have, but suddenly she knew it wouldn't make any difference. He wanted her and she knew it, and so the awareness would continue. No matter if she sat right next to him or if an entire rodeo arena separated them.

Even more important, she wanted to sit next to

him. To enjoy the feeling of being wanted by a man she'd dreamed of night after night. A feeling that would be all too brief. Once Cole realized she'd lied to him, that she was no better than his father who'd promised to take care of him, or the world that had turned its back on him. She could kiss goodbye a warm place in his memory. She would be just one of the masses that he distrusted with such fervor.

But until then she could simply enjoy being with him. Talking to him.

Besides, it wasn't as if anything could actually happen between them. Not with an arena full of people surrounding them. Which meant Nikki was safe from her raging hormones.

She slid her hand into Cole's.

SHE KNEW COLE was a big-time rodeo star. Everybody in town did, but since he'd been born and raised, nobody really paid much attention.

You're always seventeen in your hometown.

The song was true. Because while he'd been big stuff back in Lost Gun, she hadn't realized how big until she stood on the sidelines at the fairgrounds and watched Cole give a pep talk to a group of two dozen kids ranging in age from eight to eleven. A small-town reporter hung just to his left, jotting down everything he said and moving in to ask questions just as soon as he'd clapped every kid on the shoulder and wished them luck.

The reporter asked him about everything from the upcoming finals in Vegas, to his work with Boy Scouts of America.

While Nikki had heard a few tidbits circulating around town about his philanthropic efforts, most people preferred to talk about his exploits with every buckle bunny from here to Dallas. Gossip was always more fun than the truth.

Unless the truth involved a hunky cowboy with a big heart.

"You're really something," she told him when he finished posing for a few pictures and took her hand so that they could head for the tent where the pickle competition was being judged.

"No, I'm not. I'm just a man doing what needs to be done."

"Not everyone would think that."

"Not everyone had a dick for a father." He shrugged. "I'm just doing what Pete did for me. No more, no less."

But it was still enough to send a burst of warmth through her as he took her hand and they walked side by side to the tent. Like they were a real couple.

They weren't, she reminded herself.

He wasn't the loving husband and she wasn't the loving wife. He was a bad boy, and she was a wannabe bad girl, and their "arrangement" was very, very temporary.

She knew that, but damned if she didn't want to touch him anyway. As if he were the man of her dreams and this were the right moment and she could actually act on her feelings.

As if.

But this was Cole Chisholm and she was Nikki Barbie, and it would never, ever work.

If only she didn't keep forgetting that all-important fact.

11

IF HE DIDN'T TOUCH her soon he was going to lose his freakin' mind. That knowledge weighed on Cole as he scribbled down his last score—a winning number for Mrs. Earline Walker's Bread and Butter Pickle Perfection—and downed a glass of iced sweet tea someone had set in front of him. The cool liquid slid down his throat, but it did little to douse the fire that raged inside of him.

He'd been at it for three hours. Playing the dutiful husband by sitting next to her. Sliding his arm around her every now and then. Smiling and flirting and talking even, particularly during the small breaks while the person in charge of the contest rustled up the next batch of pickles. He'd actually been surprised at how easy the conversation flowed, as if they were really and truly friends, and not just pretending. He'd gotten an earful about her final class and the prep leading up to her exam at the end of the following week, and he'd filled her in on the demanding PR schedule that waited for him once he hit Vegas for the finals. On how he hated doing the standard meet and greet with the rodeo officials, but loved meeting with the local charities. Which was why he'd set up five different events, everything from laser tag with a local Boy Scout troop to horseback lessons with the orphans living at Nevada's Boysville.

Talking about his personal business wasn't something he did very often, and never with anyone other than his brothers or Eli. Oddly enough, he didn't feel the usual trepidation. The wariness.

Instead, it felt easy. Right.

She'd stared at him, her eyes full of understanding and compassion, and just like that, he'd felt less anxious. Relaxed, even. Because she knew what it was like to worry about appearances. She spent her life doing just that, just like he did.

As soon as the thought struck, he pushed it back out. He didn't worry over appearances. He just didn't like putting his business out there, opening himself up. Not because of the fear of repercussions. Hell, no. He was simply a private person.

"If I don't ace my final, I'll have to repeat the class."

"You'll nail it," he heard himself say, and he believed it. While she might be hiding behind her clothes, she still had courage. Drive. Determination.

He couldn't help but admire her as much as he liked her.

Like, he reminded himself. That's all it was. All it would ever be.

Well, that and a healthy dose of lust. He felt that in spades. Not that he was acting on it.

He reminded himself of that over the next hour as they finished the competition, awarded the trophies and ribbons, and sampled a hoard of baked goods thanks to the ladies' auxiliary.

"You've just got to try my pecan-caramel tart," said a blue-haired old woman in a pink apron emblazoned with the words *Caramel Cuties* in zebra print. "There's three of us on the baking team, but this is my own secret recipe."

"Is not, Norma Jean Daughtry," said a tiny woman with white curls and a matching apron. "I'm the one who told you to add an extra teaspoon of cinnamon and just a hint of ginger."

"In your dreams, Louise Lou," said the third member of the team. Her white hair had been piled high in a massive beehive and her cat's-eye glasses were the same pink as her apron. "I'm the one who came up with the ginger. And the pie-crust base—"

"It's obviously a team effort," Cole cut in, scooping a forkful and loading it into his mouth. "Why,

I can't wait to try the rest of these." He motioned to the table laden with various pies and cakes that the team had submitted and suddenly the argument was forgotten as the three women blushed and fell all over themselves to dish him up more goodies.

When they finally made their way back to his Jeep, Cole's hands overflowed with bakery boxes. A good thing because it kept them too busy to reach out and take Nikki's hand as they walked.

"That went well," she said as she climbed into the car. "Although you'll probably gain fifty pounds if you even attempt to eat all of that."

"Don't worry about me, sugar. I get more than my fair share of exercise." And he knew just how to burn up the extra calories.

The thought struck as she stared back at him, her eyes glittering in the dusky shadows, her lips curved into a knowing smile.

"I'll bet you do," she murmured before she seemed to catch herself. "This is a nice vehicle."

She trailed her hand over the black leather seat and Cole felt the stroke down his spine. His hands tightened on the steering wheel. *Easy, bud.*

"I bought it last year…" They spent the next few minutes talking about his Jeep while Florida Georgia Line belted out lyrics about rolling down windows and cruising around. Blake Shelton came on next singing a twangy number about jacked-up trucks and red-dirt roads and ice-cold beer, and the subject shifted to the mountain of bakery boxes.

"You can't possibly eat all of that without slipping into a diabetic coma."

"I can if I pace myself. Besides, a little sugar never hurt anybody."

"That's what my grammy used to say."

He expected her to stiffen up the way she usually did when she mentioned the old woman, but instead, she stared out the window and tapped her fingers on the dashboard. "She had a ton of euphemisms," she added. "Like 'if you can't say something nice, don't say it at all.' And 'for every finger you point, there are three pointed back at you.' Stuff like that."

"Sound advice. The best Jesse could ever come up with was 'keep your mouth shut and it will all be over soon.'" He wasn't sure why he told her. He didn't talk about his past with anyone other than his brothers. But there was something lulling about the wind whipping through the window and the engine humming in the background, mingling with the music drifting from the radio. The moon shone big and bright overhead, bathing the interior of the Jeep in a celestial light that made the entire moment seem almost surreal. As if this were just a dream. Temporary. Safe. "He usually said that when my dad was on a drinking binge. He wasn't the nicest guy then, not that he was much to speak of when he was sober, either. But he got even meaner when he was drinking. Jesse would sneak us out the back door and we would hide out in the Chevy in the driveway until he calmed down or passed out."

"How long did that take?"

"Let's just say I woke up with pins and needles too many times to count from being cooped up in that backseat."

"Which explains why you're claustrophobic."

"I'm not claustrophobic."

She motioned to the open Jeep, the top stuffed into the backseat. "This, and you've got an RV with skylights. Trust me, you're claustrophobic."

"I just like my space." He chanced a glance in the rearview mirror at the empty stretch of dirt road behind them and the knot in his stomach eased just a little. "There's nothing wrong with that."

He expected her to argue, to press home the point, but instead she fell silent for the next few moments as they roared down the road, gravel spewing, the wind whipping through the open top.

"That must have been hard," she finally murmured. He gave her a questioning glance and she added, "Growing up with so much instability. My mom was a ballbuster, but we always had a bed to sleep in and food to eat, albeit greasy and fast."

His stomach hollowed out at the memory of all

those cold, dark, hungry nights before he stiffened. "It was at first, but then we got used to it."

"Why didn't you tell anyone?"

"Who? The teachers? They would have taken us away, split us up, maybe even sent us to different towns. All we had was each other. We needed to stay together, and we did."

"I'm sorry you had to go through all of that. No kid should have to endure so much."

He'd heard the words from various people over the years, but he'd never actually believed it. Most people said as much to be polite, to ease their own conscience because they'd grown up never knowing what real strife meant.

But when Nikki opened her mouth, he actually believed her. Not because she'd endured the exact same situation, but because she'd known the same isolation. She'd spent a lifetime stuck in her sisters' shadows, hiding, fearful of discovery much the way he and his brothers had been fearful of being split apart.

He could hear it in the conviction in her voice. See it in the sincerity gleaming in her eyes. And he felt it when she leaned across to where one of his hands rested on the gear shift and covered his fingers with her own.

A soft pat that meant little in the big scheme of things, but still the tightness in his chest eased just a fraction.

He drew a deep breath. "Like I said, we're here now. That's all that matters."

"So you're not angry with your dad?"

"I don't care enough to be angry." He forced his hands to relax on the steering wheel. "He was a liar and a cheat. He doesn't deserve my anger, or anything else."

"It's okay, you know," she said after a long, contemplative moment.

"What is?"

"For you to love him. It's okay. My mother isn't the warmest woman, but she's still my mother. I love her even if I don't think she loves me sometimes." She licked her lips. "Or at all."

"She doesn't deserve your love."

"Maybe not, but that doesn't change the fact that I feel it."

"It should." That's what he said, but he wasn't so sure he believed it anymore. Not with her sitting so close and sounding so sure. "So spill. What do you have against pecan-caramel tarts?"

"Excuse me?"

He motioned to the boxes. "Or apple fritters. Or cherry cobbler. Or any of the other homemade desserts sitting in these boxes. I thought you were going to have a coronary when the ladies started loading them up."

"I just hate to see anything go to waste."

"So eat it."

"I told you, I'm specializing in more refined flavors. I don't want to kill my palate with all this stuff. It's too simple."

"There's nothing wrong with simple."

"If you're entering a small-town-fair baking contest. I want to play in the big leagues. This stuff wouldn't stand a chance, so there's no sense wasting my time or my palate on it."

"Is that so?"

"It's the truth."

"You know what I think?"

"No, but I'm sure you're going to tell me."

"I think you're afraid if you take even one bite, you'll want another despite the fact that it's simple. Because there's nothing wrong with simple." Simple and sweet and pure.

"What makes you so sure?"

He'd had one bite of her and all he could think about was another. And another. And *another*.

Because she was the one thing he couldn't have, he reminded himself. It had nothing to do with the fact that he suspected she was a helluva lot more pure beneath the surface that she let on, and damned if he didn't like it.

He didn't.

He liked his women experienced and worldly and temporary. And while Nikki looked the part, he couldn't shake the feeling that she wasn't all she was cracked up to be.

No, he wanted her so bad not because she was different from all the other women in his past, but because she didn't want him back. She was the one thing he couldn't have and so it made sense that he would be so infatuated with her. He had no doubt that one night would kill his curiosity and he could get back to thinking about Vegas and his record-breaking win.

If she'd been the least bit obliging.

She wasn't and so he intended to do his damnedest to respect her wishes.

"That was fun," she told him when they climbed out of the Jeep and he followed her to the RV. Moths flitted around the porch light, casting dancing shadows across Nikki's pale blond hair. Her eyes were rich and warm, and his heart kicked up a beat.

"It wasn't too bad." He reached for the door handle, slid the key in the lock and hauled open the door. He motioned her inside and tried to ignore the warmth that rolled through him when her arm brushed his.

"I guess I'll see you later," she said once they were inside. "I should call it a night."

He nodded. "Hopefully she'll make a move early and we can move out."

"Hopefully. Sleep tight." She stepped inside her bedroom and started to close the door. "Cole?"

He turned, his lips parted and ready—

"I really like the ring." She smiled, her luscious mouth parting to reveal a row of straight white teeth. "I know it's not real, but it's still beautiful."

Pure satisfaction somersaulted through him and he found himself grinning before he could stop himself. "A beautiful ring for a beautiful woman."

And he meant it.

At that moment, she was just about the most beautiful thing he'd ever seen. Better than any championship buckle. Or an arena full of screaming fans, or a wide-open Texas sky.

Before he could dwell on that startling thought, her soft voice drew his attention. "No man's ever given me anything before," she added, almost as an afterthought. As if she didn't want to admit the truth to him but couldn't help herself. "You're the first."

And I'll be the last.

The notion stuck as he gave her a quick peck on the lips, but then he bypassed her and walked the few feet toward his own bedroom before he said "to hell with it" and tossed Nikki on the nearest horizontal surface. Closing the door behind him, he pulled off his clothes and headed straight into an ice-cold shower.

12

NIKKI WASN'T GOING to think about Cole. Or the way he looked. Or the way he smelled. Or the fact that he was sleeping in the room right next to hers.

That's what she told herself as she lay in the comfortable bed in Cole's RV and stared at the ceiling.

Comfortable, as in she should be sleeping right now. It was midnight and she was exhausted. She'd spent the past four hours since they'd come back to the RV working on the pastry crust for her wellington while Cole had taken a shower and holed up in his bedroom to watch NASCAR and wait until her mother made the next move.

She fought down a wave of guilt for not divulging her theory.

But then that's all it was. Just a theory. It's not like she *knew* Raylene's whereabouts with dead certainty. She was going off their last conversation and a hunch, and both could be totally wrong. Why, her mother might take a turn off her current path and head for Austin or Houston. She might even cross the state line into Louisiana. The possibilities were endless and so Cole was right to wait for the next credit card transaction.

Meanwhile, she'd whipped up the perfect puff pastry—to the point that her arms ached—and retreated to the safety of her room long before he'd come back, and so she felt extremely pleased with herself. *Comfortable* plus *exhausted* plus *pleased* usually equaled a decent night's sleep.

Not this time.

Not with her lips still tingling from his chaste kiss or the image that had followed firmly entrenched in her brain.

She'd gone back into the kitchen to put away the boxes of goodies he'd brought back from the fairgrounds, and run smack-dab into him as he'd been coming out of the bathroom. She could still see him dripping wet and half-naked wearing nothing but a towel. He'd stared back at her, a handsome smile on his face, his eyes glittering with a light that said he knew how uptight he was making her. And he liked it.

Because he still wanted her.

And she wanted him.

More so now that they were pretending to be married. And spending more time together. And talking.

Her eyes snapped open and she stared at the ceiling again. She rolled onto her left side and gathered the pillow underneath her cheek, stuffing it close and snuggling down. She was going to sleep this time.

Really.

It was time to close her eyes and forget him and his fluffy white towel and knowing gaze and sexy grin.

Even more, she was going to ditch the memory of the heat in his fingertips when he'd brushed against her while sliding by to open the fridge and snag a white bakery box containing a cherry pie. She'd been surprised by the gesture and startled by the contact and amazed at her fierce response....

Her skin prickled and her eyes popped open. She rolled onto her right side and stuffed the edge of the pillow under her chin. A few wiggles and she found a good spot. One where she could surely fall deep into another world and forget all about the way he'd looked leaning against the counter, forking cherry pie into his mouth.

And the way he'd smelled, an intoxicating mixture of sweet, ripe cherries and a dangerous wildness that told her he was far more intoxicating and addictive than the most decadent of desserts should she indulge in even the smallest taste....

Her nostrils flared and she threw herself onto her stomach. Stuffing her head under the pillow, she held the edges down tight, burying herself in total blackness. Unfortunately, there was plenty of light in her head and his image was too firmly fixed. She saw him in the bright morning light streaming past the RV blinds. The broadness of his shoulders within the small confines of the RV. The bulging muscles of his massive arms. The tight ripple of his thighs as he'd walked away from her. The ever-so-slight sway of white cotton around his waist. The glimpse of one sinewy, hair-dusted thigh as the towel pushed and pulled to the side—

Her eyes popped open and she flipped onto her back. Shoving the pillow under her head, she stared at the ceiling. A sharp ache echoed between her legs and her heart raced and her tummy trembled and… Geez, who was she trying to kid? Falling asleep right now was about as likely as her pulling out her grammy Ruth's old recipes.

She sat up and climbed out of the bed. A few steps and she found herself in the small hallway that ran the length of the RV. The hardwood floor was cool beneath her bare feet but it did nothing to ease the fire burning inside her as she turned toward the right and took three steps. She stood poised outside his door.

Now what?

Just knock already.

She would, and then she would go inside. And then she would tell him that she couldn't stop thinking about him. About how much she wanted a real orgasm with an actual man and could he please, please, *please* give her one.

Just one teeny, tiny one to satisfy her curiosity and sate her lust. Then she could stop thinking about it. Fantasizing. *Hoping.*

She reached for the doorknob.

"Can't sleep?" The deep, husky timbre of his voice stirred the hair on the back of her neck and drew her around.

She found him standing at the opposite end of the RV, in the main living area. The sight of him wearing nothing but a pair of snug, faded jeans snatched her breath for a long moment and reminded her again why cohabitating with him was such a bad idea.

Soft denim cupped his crotch and molded to his lean hips and strong thighs. The button at his waist sat undone, the zipper pulled up just enough to allow a hint of modesty. But just a hint. The vee sat tantalizingly low, piquing her curiosity and stirring the sudden urge to drop to her knees, grab the zipper with her teeth and pull it south...

Ugh. For a closet good girl, she sure was having naughty thoughts.

If only the thoughts could translate into actual actions. They might, but they might not. History was not on her side, after all, and so she stiffened against the desperate urge and kept her feet planted firmly on the floor.

Still, her eyes weren't nearly as restrained and she found herself looking at the frayed rip in the denim on his right upper thigh which gave her a tantalizing glimpse of dark, silky hair and tanned muscle and... Yowza.

She'd seen him without a shirt on that first night back at her apartment, but the encounter had been so brief and frenzied that she hadn't actually had the chance to study him. And then, on the following morning when he'd been asleep on her couch, she'd been afraid to linger too long lest she wake him. The story continued on the RV. She'd catch a brief glimpse here and there when he came out of the shower or pulled off his shirt to climb into bed. But she'd never really had the opportunity to *look*.

His shoulders were broad, his arms thick and corded with muscle. Dark hair sprinkled his chest before narrowing to a funnel that bisected his ripped abdomen and disappeared beneath the half done zipper. Her gaze riveted on the hard bulge beneath the denim of his crotch and her mouth went dry.

"You hungry?" he asked.

"You have no idea."

A warm chuckle vibrated along her nerve endings. "Me, too." He held up a toasted sandwich. The aroma of melted cheese and rich butter slid into her nostrils. Her stomach grumbled despite the fact that she'd eaten enough pickles to last a lifetime.

But then pickles weren't all that satisfying.

Not like a pecan-caramel tart or a scrumptious cherry pie.

She ditched the thought and eyed him. "I can't believe you've got any room left over after cleaning out that last bakery box."

"That was good, but I need something that sticks to the ribs," he said, cutting into her thoughts and drawing her back to the all-important fact that her stomach was still grumbling. "Some real food." He motioned to the slice of cellophane-wrapped diary in his hand. "It's just plain old American cheese, but it hits the spot." She didn't miss the challenge that simmered in the bright violet depths of his eyes. As if the offer had little to do with plain, old-fashioned comfort food and everything to do with him. As if he couldn't wait to see which she picked.

Yeah, right.

It was a late-night snack. End of story. It's not like he'd stripped naked and asked—no, *begged*—her to jump his bones.

Not yet.

She stifled a wave of excitement and focused on

her grumbling stomach. It was a sandwich. Nothing more.

That's what she told herself.

She just wasn't so sure she believed it.

He was an idiot.

That was the only explanation for the fact that he'd just offered to make her a sandwich when what he really needed to do was get the hell away as fast as possible.

They had an agreement.

No sex.

That meant *no sex*. Under any circumstances. No thinking about it. No wanting it. No doing it. *No.*

Even if she did look good enough to eat nice and slow and he'd been thinking about her ever since they'd come home and he'd tried to satisfy the hunger twisting his gut with all that cherry pie.

Enough to make any man seriously ill. Except that Cole wasn't just any man. He was an uptight, hard-up, horny man, and so the pie hadn't come close to easing the gnawing in his gut. He needed something much more substantial for that.

And you think a grilled cheese is going to do the trick?

He didn't, but he had to try something.

Anything.

Otherwise…

He squelched the thought and focused on unwrapping the cheese rather than staring at the picture she made framed in the hallway.

He'd expected her to wear a slinky leopard-print bra-and-pantie set or a sheer, see-through black number or a skimpy red-hot teddy, or something equally sinful when climbing beneath the covers. The last thing he anticipated was a pair of yellow boxers with hot-pink smiley faces and a matching T-shirt.

Not that he liked hot-pink smiley faces. Not at this point in his life. He liked his women hot and spicy and temporary. Nikki looked just the opposite with her hair pulled back in a simple braid and her face scrubbed free of the heavy eye makeup and dark red lipstick that she usually wore. She looked so different, which should have killed the attraction.

It didn't.

For all her boldness, he was no longer buying her act. There were too many inconsistencies for him to really believe she was as experienced as she made out to be. That initial gasp of surprise when he'd first kissed her. The way her skin quivered ever so slightly beneath his touch. The way she'd retreated that first night at her apartment, as if running out of pure fear rather than a stroke of good judgment.

Innocent.

And so not his type.

He held tight to the knowledge, stiffened against

the ache vibrating low in his belly and reached for two slices of bread.

"No butter for me," she added when he reached for the small tub sitting on the counter.

"You can't have a grilled cheese without butter."

She smiled as if she had a secret and he prodded, "What?"

"Nothing. It's just that's what my grandmother used to say."

"She's a smart woman."

"She was." She seemed far away for a split second. "She died when I was eight. She lived in the kitchen."

"That's where you get it from."

She shook her head. "I'm a totally different type of cook. I don't do comfort food."

"What's wrong with comfort food?"

"Nothing. I mean, it's great every now and then, but I can't build a career around it. I've got to think outside the box if I want to move into a fine-dining restaurant. I sent an application into The Savoy. They have a sous-chef position open and I really want it." When he didn't say anything, she rushed on, "It's this upscale restaurant in downtown Houston that specializes in modern American food."

"I know what it is. I've been there."

"You've been to The Savoy?"

"Just because I bust my ass in a rodeo arena doesn't mean I can't clean up and rub elbows with

130 Texas Outlaws: Cole

the higher-ups. I had dinner there last month with a marketing executive from the Western wear company that sponsors me. It was pretty decent." He handed her a paper plate. "But nothing compares to this." He winked. "Except maybe peanut butter and jelly."

"So you like PB and J?" She eyed him as he slid into the seat opposite her.

"Who doesn't?" He took a sip from the glass of milk in front of him. When she didn't answer, he murmured, "Really? You don't like peanut butter?"

"It's not that I don't like it." She shrugged. "It's just not something that I eat."

"Why not?"

"Because there aren't too many fine-dining recipes that call for peanut butter and so it's just not something that I keep in stock." Regret gleamed in her eyes. "That, and old habits."

"What's that supposed to mean?"

"My mother and my grandmother didn't have the closest relationship. My mom resented my grammy Ruth because she thought she was weak. My grandfather cheated a lot and instead of booting him out on his ass, she just took it. Anyhow, when she passed on, my mother was determined to bury her memory and so she outlawed any and all of my grammy's favorites. No homemade chocolate cake. No mouthwatering mac and cheese. No ooey gooey peanut-butter-and-jelly bars."

"I think I'm getting hungry again."

Her full lips hinted at a smile. "My mom kept our kitchen pretty much bare except for TV dinners and junk food."

"But you're a chef."

"A fine-dining chef. What I prepare is a far cry from any of the recipes in my grammy's recipe box." Regret flashed in her gaze and he had the distinct feeling that she missed those recipes a lot more than she wanted to admit.

"What was your favorite?"

"I don't remember," she said. She focused on taking a bite of her sandwich and then another, as if the monotonous action could cover up the fact that she'd just lied to him.

It didn't. It just made it that much more obvious.

"My dad never cooked much when we were young." He wasn't sure why he said it. He did his damnedest to avoid thinking about the past. But with her sitting so close and looking so uneasy, he had the sudden urge to ease the tension between them. "Jesse did all the cooking. When there was food, that is."

"I'm sorry."

"Don't be. It's all water under the bridge now. The past is the past."

"And yet you're trying to stir it up by returning a bunch of money to a town that probably won't appreciate it in the first place."

"I'm not stirring anything up. This is important to Jesse. He wants to lay the past to rest. I'm already fine with it."

She took another bite and eyed him. "Are you?" she finally asked. "Because it seems to me you sound more uptight than *fine*."

But he wasn't uptight. He was scared.

The minute the thought struck, he stomped it back into the dust. He wasn't afraid of the past. Of the memories that crept into his dreams late at night. The images of his no-good father who'd promised time and time again to straighten up and make things right.

No, he was wary.

His father had made too many false promises before he'd robbed that bank and set himself on fire. He'd been a terrible parent, but he had taught Cole one important thing—people would lie their ass off to get what they wanted.

They'd lie to themselves. To others.

Which was why Cole didn't take anyone—other than his brothers and Pete—at face value.

Actions spoke louder than words, and so he paid more attention to what people did rather than what they said.

Case in point—Nikki might talk the talk when it came to being a bona fide bad girl, but she wasn't walking the walk. At least not at the moment.

An act to convince him she wasn't his type and turn him off completely?

If so, it sure as hell wasn't working.

She looked so innocent and sweet sitting across from him, so opposite of the kind of woman he always went for, and damned if he didn't want to reach out anyway.

Because she was sweet and innocent and still the same girl who'd eyed him with such trust and slipped her hand into his all those years ago.

He shifted, eager to kill the dangerous thought. "So The Savoy, huh?"

"If they'll have me. If not, I've got applications out at two other restaurants—The Bistro and Michael's. Whatever happens, it'll be great because I'll be doing what I love."

"Will you?" He eyed the empty plate in front of her. "That's the first time I've seen you eat more than a few bites of anything."

"I had a light dinner."

"My point exactly. You nibble and taste but you don't dig in. Maybe you ought to pull out a few of those recipes every now and then."

She looked as if she wanted to argue, but then she shrugged. "My gram did make a pretty mean grilled cheese. She used honey. Just a dab, but enough to make it melt-in-your-mouth. Not that yours wasn't good. It was. I really enjoyed it." She eyed what was left of his sandwich.

He motioned to his plate. "Be my guest."

"Oh, no, I can't do that."

"It's my second one. I'm full."

"Really?"

He nodded and she reached over so fast that the plate slid a few inches. A grin tugged at his lips. "I could make you another if you want."

"No," she said around a mouthful. "This is plenty."

He watched her finish off his sandwich and marveled at the sudden feeling of companionable silence that engulfed them for the next few moments.

"Wow. I am so full," she finally remarked. Her gaze collided with his. "Maybe I can return the favor and cook for you sometime."

He thought of the pungent truffle oil, and the dozen other ingredients she'd toted onto his bus for study purposes and shook his head. "Help me get my money back and we'll call it even."

The hope in her eyes faded. "I'm really sorry about what happened. I never thought…" She shook her head. "I didn't realize she was that desperate. I guess I was too busy hiding out in the kitchen."

"And putting on one hell of a show." He wasn't sure why he called her out on it. She would deny it. He knew that.

But he asked anyway because deep down, he

hoped she would tell him the truth. That she would be different from everyone else. Honest. Trustworthy.

"What's that supposed to mean?"

"That I suspect you're not half as wild and bold as you pretend to be."

"I am so."

"Yeah?" He gave her a knowing look. "Nice boxer shorts."

She glanced down as if realizing what she was wearing for the first time. She looked so distraught that he had the sudden urge to step forward and pull her into his arms.

Her expression quickly faded into a frown. "My leather teddy was dirty tonight."

"That's too bad." He slid out from the table and she followed. "But if it makes you feel any better, you look even better in the boxers."

He didn't mean to step toward her. He was supposed to walk the other way and put as much distance as possible between them. He knew that, but he couldn't seem to help himself.

He stopped just shy of touching her. Her heat curled toward him, begging him closer. He pressed a kiss to her forehead before turning toward the door. It was that or kiss her smack-dab on her full lips, which he was dangerously close to doing.

"Dr. Pepper cake," she blurted out as he reached the doorway.

He glanced over his shoulder.

"My favorite recipe of Gram's. It's Dr. Pepper cake," she said, surprising him even more than if she'd stripped bare and jumped him right there in the hallway. "It's this old recipe handed down through about five generations. She used to make it every year for my birthday." And then she turned and disappeared into her bedroom, leaving him even more uptight than he'd been when he'd first headed into the kitchen.

For whatever reason, she'd told him the truth.

He knew it, felt it, and damned if it didn't bother him.

Because he liked it.

He liked knowing that she trusted him enough to share a piece of her past.

At the same time, they were just words. They didn't mean anything because true or not, she was still holding back when it came to the rest of her life. Still putting up a front and pretending to be something she wasn't.

And she would still walk away when all was said and done.

And damned if that didn't bother him more than anything.

SHE'D EATEN A pecan-caramel tart and two peach turnovers.

She hadn't planned it. But lack of sleep and desperate hormones had finally gotten the best of her and she found herself up at 6:00 a.m., raiding the refrigerator and praying with all of her heart that Cole didn't wake up and catch her.

Not that it mattered.

She knew what she'd done.

She stared at the bakery box with only a few crumbs left inside and satisfaction ripped through her. Her tongue tingled and her taste buds sang and damned if she didn't want to eat more.

"I knew you had it in you." The deep voice slid down her spine and she stiffened.

"I…" What could she say? For all her talk about refined taste buds, she was still the same girl who'd licked the bowl after her grandmother all those years ago. Shy. Timid. Living in the shadows of both her sisters.

She was, but Cole Chisholm didn't know that. Sure, he suspected, but he didn't *know*.

"I think we've got raccoons," she blurted, tossing the empty box in the trash and marching back to her room.

"A blonde raccoon." His deep voice followed her, and she knew he didn't just suspect, he knew.

Hardly.

He might think he had her all figured out, but he had another think coming. She wasn't just going to give up the facade and trade in her miniskirts for the sweats packed in her suitcase because Cole Chisholm thought he knew her.

He might be convinced she was sweet and wholesome and innocent, but she knew plenty of ways to prove him wrong.

And there was no better time to start than right now.

14

FOR THE FIRST time in a long time, Cole Chisholm was alone on a Friday night.

He sat at the bar, a bottle of beer in front of him, a lively two-step number bouncing off the walls around him.

The small honky-tonk sat just off the highway on the outskirts of Three Rivers, a postage-stamp-size town that played to sportsmen with its rolling acres of prime hunting ground. It was just a few weeks into deer season and so the area was crawling with men. More men meant that the local women came out in droves.

All he had to do was scope out the sea of hot bodies that filled the dance floor and pick whichever one caught his fancy. A blonde bombshell with big breasts or a brunette with a nice ass or a redhead with long legs. Someone to take the edge off and ease the damn near constant hard-on making his life freakin' miserable. A good lay and he would stop fantasizing about Nikki.

Then he could think again.

Concentrate.

At the same time there was nothing wrong with pacing himself. He had all night, and so instead of eyeballing a woman he settled for a beer.

He took a deep swig of Coors, but the liquid didn't ease the tightening in his gut or sate the thirst that clawed at his throat.

So get to it.

He should. But damned if he could make himself move. Instead, he downed another swig of beer and wished with all his heart that he could punch something.

His gaze fixed on the woman currently two-stepping her way across the dance floor with another man.

His woman.

She wore a short black leather fringe vest that didn't have anything underneath except smooth, silky skin and a pair of black leather pants that hung low on her hips. Add a pair of blinged-out cowboy boots and Nikki Barbie was definitely the hottest thing in this joint.

But her appeal went deeper than the sexy getup. Her long blond hair was slightly mussed and flowed down around her shoulders. Her eyes sparkled. Her skin glowed. She looked as if she'd just rolled out of bed after a night of incredible sex.

Yeah, right.

She'd built such a fortified wall between them that sex wasn't even a remote possibility. Hell, he'd barely kissed her since that first night.

No, the only thing they'd been doing was talking and sharing and spending time together.

And damned if that didn't make him feel that much more twisted inside. Because he liked spending time together, even if they weren't having sex.

Because they weren't.

Because Cole Chisholm wanted more than sex from her.

He ditched the last thought, downed another gulp and barely resisted the urge to haul ass across the room and inform her that she was making a fool of herself.

Why, she was hanging all over that guy.

Her arms looped around his neck. A smile tilted her full lips as she drank in his every word. She slid this way and that, her boots kicking up sawdust as she danced and lived up to her infamous Barbie reputation.

So much for feeling like the black sheep of the family. Naive? Innocent?

Like *hell*.

She looked sexy and wanton, and completely oblivious to Cole.

Not that he cared. Hell, no. So what if she didn't want to have sex with him? She was entitled to her opinion.

But they were still friends.

Even more, they were supposed to be married.

She was his wife, for Pete's sake. The least she could do was look at him.

And if she doesn't know you're here?

That thought bothered him even more than the notion that she just didn't want to acknowledge him.

While they hadn't actually slept together, they'd become so close. He could still feel her soft, voluptuous curves pressed up against him. He could hear the frantic breaths that sawed past her lips and the excited beat of her heart. He could smell the intoxicating aroma of warm, sweet woman. Her memory haunted him.

Because she was different. What he felt was different.

Like what Jesse felt for Gracie.

And what Billy felt for Sabrina.

A pang of envy shot through him. One he quickly ignored by downing the rest of his beer. He wasn't Jesse. Or Billy. They'd both come through the past and turned out to be better men for it. Jesse was so responsible now, and Billy who'd never been able to make his mind up when it came to a woman, had actually become decisive.

But Cole…

He'd never been comfortable in any one situation for too long. Not when he'd been trapped in the backseat of that beat-up, rusted car when he'd been just a kid and not now when the walls of the RV closed in and he needed to breathe. He liked knowing there were no ties. That he could just pick up and leave and not worry about looking back.

Yep, Jesse and Billy didn't mind looking back, but Cole didn't see the point, and he never would.

It was all about moving forward.

Soon they would catch up to Raylene, recover the money and then he would head for Vegas. Nikki and their "marriage" would become just another part of the past he kept buried.

All the more reason to get his ass out of here. The way she'd felt and the way he'd felt and the fact that they'd become so close was over and done with.

Time to focus on the here and now.

As if on cue, he felt a tap on his shoulder. He put on his most charming grin and turned to see the woman who'd come up behind him. She was sex on a stick, with pretty pouty lips and long dark hair and a curvy figure.

Perfect for a night of hot, wild, mindless sex.

"How about you buy me a drink?"

"I'd love to, but I'm here with someone."

"What?"

Yeah, what?

He motioned across the dance floor. "She's running late."

"Well, if you get tired of waiting." She winked. "I'll be here."

She walked away and he signaled the bartender to bring him a second round before shifting his gaze back to Nikki.

The minute his attention fixed on her, she stiffened and missed a step. She teetered and the man caught her. His hands slithered around her waist and he pulled her close and—

No.

Hell, no.

He pushed to his feet and, just like that, Cole gave in to a fierce swell of possessiveness. Regardless of what had—or, in this case, hadn't happened in the past, right now, at this moment, Nikki was his.

He knew it.

She knew it.

And it was high time she admitted it.

Uh-oh.

Panic bolted through Nikki because it wasn't supposed to happen this way. He wasn't supposed to waltz over to her. No, he was supposed to give up any notions about the two of them and head for the nearest available female.

Instead, he was walking straight for her.

She ignored the urge to bolt for the nearest exit—a confident sex kitten did not run—and tightened her hold on the man's neck—Jimmy or Joe or John or something such with a J—and stared into his eyes. And kept swaying. And smiling.

The trouble was, she didn't have to look to know that Cole was headed straight for her. She saw him out of the corner of her eye, a determined shadow that bisected the dance floor and closed the distance between them. Even more, she could feel him.

Her skin prickled and heat skittered up and down her spine. It was all she could do not to turn when he stepped up behind her.

"We need to talk." His deep voice slid into her ears, pushing aside the music and laughter and the frantic beat of her heart.

She stiffened against the urge to turn, wrap her arms around his neck and see if he tasted half as delicious as she remembered.

And then what?

That's what scared her the most. The possibility that she would do something wrong and disappoint him. And then he would turn away. Run away.

She twined her fingers around Jimmy/Joe/John's neck and gave him an apologetic smile. "As you can see, I'm kind of in the middle of something right now," she told Cole.

But Cole wasn't giving up so easily. "It'll only take a few minutes."

"I'm busy."

"I can see that." He sounded none too pleased and a traitorous slither of joy went through her. For a split second, she entertained the crazy hope that his feelings went deeper than a physical attraction. That he actually cared about her. Enough to stick around even if she wasn't the most experienced in the sack.

Crazy.

She didn't need him to stick around because she wasn't sticking around. She was out of here. On her way to Houston. To the rest of her life.

"Give me five minutes."

"And miss my favorite song?" She gave Jimmy/ Joe/John another "sorry about this" look. "I love Luke Bryan."

"This is Jason Aldean."

"Close enough."

"Look, buddy. The lady doesn't want to talk to you," Jimmy/Joe/John cut in. "So take a hike."

"I think you should take the hike."

"Like hell…" Jimmy/Joe/John stared past her and annoyance morphed to trepidation. "Well, maybe I could give you guys a minute."

"Great." Cole's deep voice sounded a split second before he took her hand.

"You can't just come in here and butt into my fun." Her voice followed him, but he didn't slow his pace as he strode toward the nearest exit. He hit the bar on the door, pushed through and headed around the building.

Where she'd avoided taking a good look at him inside, she couldn't help but look now.

He wore a black T-shirt, faded jeans and a look that said he was royally pissed. Tension rolled off his body and his jaw clenched. A muscle ticked wildly near his left cheek. His eyes had clouded to a dark, stormy violet, like the sky just before it opened up before a fierce summer rain.

She ignored the tiny thrill that slid through her and planted her hands on her hips. "Just what do you think you're doing?"

He pushed his hat back on his head and inched closer, making her crane her neck to look at him. "You're wrong. Dead wrong."

"About what?"

"About sex." His voice lowered a notch. "We're both consenting adults. You're hot and bothered and I'm hot and bothered. There's no reason why we ought to be trolling at a place like this. We should do this." He stared down at her, his eyes blazing with jealousy and a hunger that kicked her in the chest and sent the air whooshing from her lungs. "You and me."

Excitement bolted through her, followed by a rush of doubt because while she might *want* to do this, she couldn't.

Deep down, she knew she was a fake. A fraud. But knowing what a big disappointment she was in the sack and seeing it firsthand in his eyes were two very different things.

She swallowed past the sudden lump in her throat. "I really don't think—"

"That's your problem, sugar. You think too much when it's not about that. It's about this." And then his mouth swooped down and captured hers.

15

NIKKI'S HEART BEAT double-time, the sound thundering in her ears, drowning out her conscience and her fear. She slid her arms around his neck, stopped thinking altogether and just felt. The purposeful slant of his lips. The tantalizing dance of his tongue. The strong splay of his hands at the base of her spine. The muscular wall of his chest crushing her breasts. The hardness of his thighs pressed flush against hers.

His lips plundered hers, his tongue pushing deep to stroke and explore and leave her breathless. He pressed her up against the side of the building so that she could feel the pulse of the music from inside. The excitement. And then he leaned into her, his body flush against hers, so that she could feel *his* excitement.

He caught the button holding her vest together and slid open the closure. The edges fell apart and her breasts spilled free. Dipping his head, he caught one rosy nipple between his teeth. He flicked the tip with his tongue before opening his mouth wider. He drew her in and sucked until a moan vibrated up her throat. The sound fed the lust roaring in his veins. He caught the hem of her skirt and growled when he realized that she wasn't wearing any panties. Pressing one hard thigh between her legs he forced her wider until she rode him. Her sweet heat rasped against his starched denim.

She gasped and a shudder ripped through her.

He shifted, moving and rubbing, working her as he caught her lips in a fierce kiss. His hand plunged between her legs, pressing into the wet heat, and she stiffened at the rush of sweet sensation. A small cry ripped past her lips and a sizzling heat pulsed through her body before her eyelids finally fluttered open and she found him staring down at her, into her, as if seeing her for the first time. A rush of panic went through her and she turned, pressing her bottom back against him.

He let loose a growl as he noted her silent invitation. Strong fingers worked at the button on his jeans and then she felt the sag of denim. His erection sprang forward, hard and greedy, pushing against her for a split second before he pulled away.

"I need a condom," he murmured, his voice yanking her back to reality.

Of course he did. This might be her first time doing something like this, but it obviously wasn't his.

And she *was* doing it.

The petting had gone too far. No sex-loving Barbie in her right mind would back out now. If she did, he would know the truth.

And if she went through with it?

He would know the truth.

Maybe and maybe not.

They were going at it so fast and furious that maybe, just maybe he wouldn't notice the trembling in her hands or the quivering of her lips or the fact that while she knew what she wanted from him, she didn't actually know what to do.

Even more, maybe if she did it right here, right now, it wouldn't be all that great. Then she could stop thinking about doing it, fantasizing, *wanting*. Cole Chisholm would fade into her memory like the first two guys and she could get her mind back on her midterm.

She held tight to the hope while he retrieved a condom and worked it on with a speed that said he'd done it many times before.

The realization stirred a strange sense of regret. One that quickly drowned in a wave of heat as she felt the brush of knuckles against her backside as he positioned himself. His thick head nudged apart her slick folds and pressed into her.

She closed her eyes against the slight pressure of him pushing inside, stretching and filling her inch by decadent inch.

Slowly.

So sweet and incredibly slow, as if he knew that she didn't do this very often.

She stiffened and summoned her most sultry voice. "Harder," she breathed, fighting back a slight wince when he quickly obliged.

A pinch that quickly faded into a pulsing awareness as he filled her completely. Her heart paused. He throbbed and her body contracted. A tremor went through her and she fought to control the heat slip-sliding along her nerve endings, threatening her sanity and her control.

No, no, no.

The chant echoed in her head as she fought to keep from going up in flames right here and now like the novice she truly was. A woman who spent her nights fantasizing rather than doing. A woman desperate for a man's touch.

For his touch.

The hard tin vibrated against her fingertips, reminding her that she wasn't just out of her comfort zone when it came to men, but she was far, far away from the safety of her bedroom. Reality crept in, along with the sounds drifting from inside the honky-tonk. The music and the laughter and the voices…

A man's deep voice.

"Follow me, sweet cheeks, and we'll head back to my place."

Nikki felt Cole's muscles tense. Her eyes opened and her head snapped up in time to see the couple that stumbled around the side of the building and headed for the row of cars sitting nearby.

"Screw that," the woman murmured. "The back-seat is just fine by me."

Nikki held her breath as gravel crunched and metal creaked. The door slammed, but the voices still carried through the open car window.

And while Nikki couldn't see anything thanks to a nearby Dumpster that blocked the view, she could still hear them, which meant they could hear her.

The panting.

The moaning.

She reached for the edges of her vest, but Cole's hands covered hers, flattening them against the wall as he pressed his body against hers. "You're not scared of an audience, are you?"

"Who? Me?" She swallowed against her suddenly dry throat. "Of course not." It wasn't like she was buck-naked out in the open. There was a Dumpster. "I live for an audience. The more, the better."

"Then why are you so tense?"

"Mosquitoes," she blurted. "I mean, we're out in the open and I didn't use any bug spray and—"

"The only thing biting you is going to be me," he murmured, his lips grazing her ear. One hand slid up her abdomen to her breast and he caught her nipple. He pinched the ripe tip and played until need sizzled up and down her spine and the tension eased from her body. Her lips parted on a gasp.

"You'd better watch it or they'll hear you." He slid his left arm around her, his fingers skimming her rib cage as he caught her other nipple. Now both hands plucked and rolled the sensitive tips until her knees went weak.

"So?" she managed a split second before he thrust into her. Still she caught the cry that curled up her throat and clamped her mouth shut as he started to move.

In and out. Back and forth.

The backseat action going on nearby soon faded into the beat of her own heart as she arched against Cole. She drew him deeper, held him longer, until the pressure between her legs reached the breaking point. Sensation drenched her and she exploded around him. Her head fell back into the curve of his neck and a groan worked its way up her throat.

Before she could bite her lip against the sound, his mouth covered hers as he moved faster and plunged harder, deeper, stronger. Convulsions gripped him. She milked him, her slick folds clenching around his throbbing penis until a growl sizzled across her nerve endings.

He buried himself one last time and leaned into her. His body flattened hers against the brick wall. The rough slab rasped her overly sensitive nipples and desire speared her again. Every nerve in her body sizzled. She closed her eyes, relishing the aftershocks of her release which swept through her and kept the fear at bay for the next several moments. Until reality washed back in and she became aware of the skirt up around her waist and the chill night air slithering over her bare skin, and the grumble of a car engine a few feet away.

Close.

So close.

And she was back to trembling again, desperate to curl up against him, to cuddle.

"I really need to go," she blurted. "It's getting late and I need to study." She ducked underneath the arm to her left and put a few safe inches between them as she struggled with her clothes. "I had a good time. Thanks." And then she walked away because the last thing she needed was for Cole Chisholm to see the gratitude blazing in her eyes. The wonder. The damned *happiness*.

Because Nikki Barbie had had her first orgasm.

And her second. And they'd both been fan-friggin'-tastic.

Of all the rotten luck.

16

No way did she just rock his world and then just ditch him like he was last week's leftovers.

Good?

Was she delusional?

It hadn't been good. It had been great. It had been awesome. *Phenomenal*.

For him, but she obviously didn't share the feeling because she'd already climbed into the rental car and pulled out of the parking lot.

G'bye.

He ran a frustrated hand through his hair and fought the urge to follow her back to the RV. A crazy feeling because Cole Chisholm didn't chase after women. They chased after him.

And he could damn well prove it.

There was an entire bar full of females who would

have been damned happy to leave here with him.
Damned happy.

He tried to remember the half dozen or so women
who'd hit on him. Prime candidates for his Southern charm. All he had to do was walk back inside.
Smile. And bam, he would move on to the next and
forget all about Nikki.

That's what he told himself, but damned if he believed it.

Cole didn't want another woman.

He wanted Nikki Barbie.

You had her, bud.

But he didn't just want a quickie out behind the
bar. He wanted to lay her down on a soft mattress and
plunge fast and sure and deep. He wanted to pull her
close and fall asleep to the steady beat of her heart.
And then he wanted to wake up next to her and do
it all over again.

And again.

Forever? Like hell. The last thing Cole wanted
was to tie himself down for the rest of his life. He
didn't do commitment.

Just sex.

Lots of sex.

Not that he was going to go after her and say as
much. No, she'd been the one to walk away, so she
would have to be the one to make the first move
next time.

If there was a next time.

Maybe. Maybe not.

For the first time in his life, he wasn't sure.

But while he had no intention of making the first move, he had no problem dangling the bait.

She might mean to resist him from here on out, but he wasn't going to make it easy on her.

Not by a long shot.

HE WAS DRIVING her crazy.

Nikki came to that conclusion several hours later after returning to the RV. Cole came in a short while after her, and it had been constant contact ever since.

She'd run into him coming out of the shower. And scooted by him while he stood half-naked in the kitchen. And tried to whip up a cream sauce while he sat sprawled in a nearby chair, wearing nothing but a pair of jeans and a smile.

As if he knew that his closeness chipped away at her defenses.

The next day went much the same way.

He walked around the RV half-dressed and made it a point to touch her whenever she got a little too close. And he talked to her…about what she was making and what he liked to eat and how much he really enjoyed a home-cooked meal.

So?

She didn't care because she wasn't into home

cooking. She wasn't into *him,* even if she had experienced a temporary loss of sanity at the bar. She'd given in to her sexual frustration, but she didn't intend to make that mistake again.

She'd hoped to work him out of her system, but she'd failed miserably. And now she was miserable.

He was close enough to touch, to stroke, to taste, yet she couldn't do any of it because that meant forgetting her objective—get through the next few days and get on with her life without falling for Cole Chisholm.

And that's what she feared would happen.

She was too naive when it came to doing the deed, which explained the crazy feelings pushing and pulling inside of her. Like how much she liked him. And how she wished with all of her heart that he liked her.

Like, of all things.

But their relationship wasn't about like. It was strictly business. Platonic.

Which was exactly what she told her sister Crystal when the woman finally called from her honeymoon after getting word of Nikki's sudden marriage.

She'd known the phone call would come eventually. She'd just hoped to go as long as possible first.

"Platonic? You married Cole Chisholm and the relationship is strictly *platonic?*"

"Exactly." Crystal actually laughed and Nikki rushed on, "I'm serious. He needed to get the women in town off his back and I needed to get Mom off mine. We faked a ceremony and bam, everyone thinks we're together so they leave us alone."

"And there's nothing going on?"

She thought of Cole pressed up against her outside of the bar. "No," she managed, despite the sudden lump in her throat. "Nothing. Listen, I know it sounds crazy, but it worked. I had to do something when you and April jumped ship." She didn't mention the manhunt across Texas. The last thing she wanted was to ruin her sister's honeymoon and make her feel guilty because she'd followed her heart to marry the man of her dreams. "I supported you guys. Please understand about this."

"Oh, I understand. I understand that you're fake married to the hottest hunk and it's strictly platonic. What I don't understand is why? Aren't you the least bit attracted to him?"

"It's not about that."

"Maybe it should be."

"What's that supposed to mean?"

"That for the first time in your life, you've actually done something wild and crazy. You should lighten up and enjoy yourself. You're there. He's there. You don't want any strings. He doesn't want any strings. Sounds like the perfect situation to work off a little sexual frustration, and heaven knows you need that.

How long has it been since that last guy you went out with?"

"A while."

"Months?" Crystal pressed.

"Give or take a few years."

"Seriously?" Crystal let loose a low whistle. "Nikki, you need to go after Cole right now, jump his bones and have a little fun."

"I think it will complicate things." Forget *think*. She knew it would complicate things. She'd jumped his bones and now she could barely look him in the eye without desperately wanting to do it again. Talk about a major complication.

"Put on your big-girl panties and stop acting like a naive kid. Sex is the most uncomplicated thing there is. It's relationships that get complicated. Just keep things physical and enjoy yourself. You're only young once."

"I'll think about it." *Not*. "I miss you. Tell April I said hi."

"You're not changing the subject that easily."

Nikki smiled. "Oh, yes, I am. So how's Hawaii?"

_17_

HER SISTER WAS right.

Nikki came to that conclusion a half hour after she'd said goodbye to Crystal. She'd taken a cold shower, pulled on her soft cotton _Hell's Kitchen_ T-shirt and sweats, and stretched out on the bed. This was her time to be young and she should be enjoying it.

Instead, she was channel surfing and eating a cold slice of pizza.

Granted, it was a homemade gourmet pizza she'd made herself and her taste buds were singing, but still.

She glanced at the remote in one hand and the half-eaten pepperoni in the other. It was her Friday night fantasy come to life. The chance to buck her reputation and simply be herself. This was what she wanted.

Okay, so this was what she'd wanted before Cole Chisholm had rolled into her life in his big rig and screwed up her priorities. Now she wanted him. And he wanted her.

Want.

It didn't have to go beyond that if she didn't let it. If she cut herself off emotionally from the sex and kept her feelings locked up tight.

Then she could enjoy herself for the next day or so before she caught up to her mother and the shit hit the fan. Couldn't she?

She could.

She would.

She was tired of fantasizing. She wanted the real thing. The real man. Just for a little while. Deep down, she knew no matter where she went, or how many five-star restaurants she cooked at or how many award-winning chefs she learned from, she would never meet another man like Cole Chisholm.

He was one of a kind.

Her first love.

Her last.

She ignored the thought and threw her legs over the side of the bed. This wasn't about love. It was all about sex. About *having* sex.

Nikki peeled off her clothes, pulled on her sundress—minus the undies—and reached for her sandals. She glanced at the clock and entertained a rush of anxiety that quickly fed her determination.

Gathering her courage, she left the room and went looking for Cole.

She found him stretched out in a lounge chair on the top deck of his RV. A full moon hung overhead, the sky a blanket of stars that twinkled and cast an ethereal light on the cowboy who'd been starring in her most provocative fantasies.

He wore only his cowboy hat and a pair of jeans. His chest was bare, his shoulders broad. His shirt lay in a heap next to his boots. Muscles rippled as he stuffed his hands under his head and gazed up at the sky overhead.

The faint sound of music drifted from inside the RV, joining with the buzz of crickets and the pounding of Nikki's heart as she cleared the top step of the ladder and stepped up onto the roof. The bus creaked ever so slightly and Cole's head snapped up. His gaze collided with hers.

She braced herself against any lingering doubts, cleared her suddenly dry throat and murmured, "What are you doing up here?"

He tipped the brim of his hat back, lifting the veil of shadow from his face. His gaze glittered hot and bright in the moonlight. "I hate being cooped up sometimes."

"I thought you said you weren't claustrophobic."

"I'm not. It's just that me and my brothers spent one night too many sleeping in our dad's old Chevy—when he was on a drinking binge. Sometimes being inside the RV reminds me of it, so I climb up here to catch my breath." He settled back down and gazed back up at the moon. "What about you? Can't sleep?"

"Actually—" She swallowed and gathered the courage that had brought her this far. "I'm too busy thinking to sleep." Her gaze caught and held his. "I can't stop thinking about you." She stepped toward him. "About us." She dropped to her knees. "This." She leaned over and kissed him long and slow and deep, leaving no doubt how much she wanted him.

He returned her kiss, but he made no move to reach out. She leaned back just enough to murmur, "I want you, Cole," and then she took his lips in another deep, purposeful kiss. "I always did, I just didn't think you'd want me back. Not if you knew the truth."

"Which is?"

"That I wasn't half the good-time girl everyone thought." Her gaze caught and held his. "I didn't turn away from you that night because you weren't experienced enough for me. I turned away because I wasn't experienced enough. That's why I ran away. Not because I didn't want you. Because I didn't want this."

Nikki fought against one last wave of fear and then she straddled him.

18

COLE BLINKED, BUT Nikki didn't fade and disappear the way she did in his fantasies.

Because this wasn't a fantasy.

She was real. Warm. *Here.*

She sat astride him, her skin pale and silky in the moonlight. She shimmied her body and hiked her dress to her waist to give her legs some breathing room. With the material out of her way, she spread wider and settled more fully over him. Her bare sex rested atop his cock that throbbed beneath his jeans. She gripped his shoulders, stared deep into his eyes and rubbed herself against him.

She flung her head back and went wild for the next few moments and it was all he could do not to touch her smooth thighs or knead her sweet, round ass or slide his fingers into her wet heat.

But Cole had been waiting for this moment since

the night of the wedding. He'd dreamed of it. He wasn't about to hurry things up. He balled his hands into fists, braced himself and let her work herself up.

"You feel so good." She hesitated then and her gaze met his. It was all he could do not to take her in his arms and chase away the doubt. "Do you like it, too?"

"Baby, you have no idea." His words reassured her and she smiled, a brilliant slash of white in the moonlit darkness. His chest hitched and his breath caught. "You're so beautiful, Nikki."

"So are you," she murmured, her smile fading into something more primitive and determined.

She kept riding him, rubbing herself up and down, creating a delicious friction before she finally leaned back and reached for the waistband of his shorts. He was already so hard that the zipper caught and refused to budge until his hand closed over hers.

He lifted his pelvis and together they slid his zipper the rest of the way down. He pushed his jeans down, hooking his underwear along with it, until his erection sprang thick and heavy toward her. Her fingertip was hot and arousing as she traced a throbbing vein up his rock-hard length, until she reached the silky-smooth head.

Nikki had seen a few male members in her time, but none of them had been near as impressive as Cole. Bold and beautiful, his penis jutted tall, throbbing beneath her tentative touch. She circled the engorged purple head and he sucked in a breath. The sound fed her confidence and she wrapped her hand around him. Heat scorched her fingertips and he arched into her grasp. But he didn't touch her.

Not yet.

Her gaze trailed up over a ridged abdomen, a broad chest sprinkled with dark, silky hair, a corded neck, to the chiseled perfection of his face partially hidden in the shadow of his cowboy hat.

She took his hat off, set it aside and stared into his deep violet eyes. There was no mistaking the raw, aching need that gripped him.

And the uncertainty.

And the regret.

Because he'd wanted her back then.

Unlike the other boys, he hadn't been anxious to add a notch to his belt. He'd really and truly wanted her, and she'd turned her back on him.

Before she could draw another breath, his mouth covered hers and his tongue thrust between her parted lips. The kiss seemed to go on forever and when he finally pulled away, Nikki couldn't seem to catch her breath.

She fought for air while he reached down into the pocket of his jeans and retrieved a foil packet. A few seconds later, he slid the condom onto his erection, gripped her waist and pulled her closer.

He pressed his hard sex between her legs. The plump head pushed into her just a fraction until she felt her body pulse around his thick shaft. A shiver ripped through her and she slid her hands around his neck and threaded her fingers into his hair. Her nipples tightened, pressing against the thin material of her dress, and her thighs trembled.

He kissed her slowly, deeply, before he finally drew away. His heated gaze held hers as he lifted her hips again, pushing into her a fraction more. But it wasn't enough. There was still too much between them.

She braced her hands against his chest and climbed to her feet. She backed up just a few steps and reached for the edge of her dress. Bunching the hem, she pulled it up and over her head. Her nipples hardened against the sudden breeze blowing in off the water and she trembled.

Cole's gaze swept the length of her. Fire flared in his eyes, chasing away the sudden chill of self-consciousness that suddenly gripped her. There was no mistaking the emotion in his gaze as it met hers— a mixture of open hunger and fierce possessiveness that told her he wouldn't dream of walking away from her.

He accepted her.

Liked her.

Loved her.

She forced aside the ridiculous notion. She wasn't silly enough to believe there could be a happily ever after with Cole. They had different lives. Different futures.

No, this wasn't about tomorrow.

This was about right now.

She watched as he stood and shed his jeans completely. He settled back down on the lounge chair and motioned for her.

"Come here," he murmured, his voice raw and husky and oh so stirring.

Anticipation rippled through her and every nerve in her body tingled. She straddled him again, her knees and calves cushioned by the padded canvas of the chair.

She slid the swollen bud of her clitoris against his engorged penis until she reached the head. She rubbed from side to side, feeling him pulse against her most tender spot. She gasped when his teeth caught one nipple and he closed his lips over the sensitive peak. He drew her deep into his mouth and sucked so hard that she felt the tug between her legs.

She moved a fraction higher and pressed the wet opening of her body over the head of his erection. His hold on her nipple broke as a raged gasp escaped his lips. She pushed down slightly, letting him stretch her, fill her just enough to make her insides tighten, and then she withdrew.

He bucked beneath her and she did it again, pushing down just enough to make her body crave more before pulling back and gasping for air. His hands slid down her back and his large fingers pressed into her bottom as if to pull her back down. But he didn't. While he was now an active participant, this was still her ride, her chance to discover her wild side and unleash it at her own pace.

She kissed him then, sucking at his tongue the way her body grasped at the head of his erection.

Over and over.

His muscles bunched tight beneath her fingertips, his body hard and stiff beneath her, until she knew he couldn't take any more.

With a shudder, she slid down over him until she felt the base of his shaft fully against her. The soft silk of his pubic hair teased the sensitive lips of her vagina. He pulsed inside her for a long, heart-stopping moment before he gripped her bottom with both hands and his hips lifted.

He slid deeper. The sensation of being stretched and filled by the raw strength of him stalled the air in her lungs for several heart-pounding moments.

The pressure between her legs was sharp and sweet. But not half as sharp and sweet as the sudden tightening in her chest when he looked at her, his gaze so fierce and possessive, as if he never meant to let her go.

As if.

Nikki dismissed the thought and fixed her attention on the desire coiling tight in her body. She rocked her hips, riding him with an intensity that made her heart pound and her body throb.

She held his gaze with each movement, determined to brand his every expression into her memory. Until sensation gripped her, so wild and tantalizing, that her breath stalled and her heart all but stopped beating. She couldn't help herself. While she wanted to watch, the only thing she seemed capable of in that next instant was feeling. Her eyes closed. Her head fell back.

He held her tight as he pushed down around him. Her body released a warm, sucking rush of moisture. He groaned then, his hands digging into her bottom as he bucked beneath her. His eyes blazed a feverish gold. The muscles in his neck tightened as she surged one last and final time, burying himself deep as he exploded.

She collapsed against him, her head in the curve of his shoulder as she tried to catch her breath. His arms tightened around her and he simply held her then, stroking her back and her bottom as her heart slowly returned to normal.

Oddly enough, it was those stroking, soothing moments afterward that stood out in her mind long after Cole had helped her into her clothes, led her down the side of the RV and back inside. While her orgasm had been earth-shattering, what had followed had been life-changing.

Because Nikki had never felt as beautiful, as cherished, as loved as she had when Cole had cradled her beneath the stars.

She grasped the feeling close and refused to acknowledge the small voice in her head that told her she would never, ever feel that way with any other man.

It wasn't about the future. It was about making the most of the next few hours until they reached their final destination and Cole realized that she'd lied to him about knowing her mother's whereabouts.

He would go back to distrusting her and she would go back to denying her feelings, and they would both return to their separate lives. He would head for the next rodeo and she would pack her bags for Houston, and that would be that.

The end.

But not yet. They still had a little bit of time and she intended to make the most of it and store as many memories as possible.

19

COLE HAD BARELY opened the door of the RV when Nikki backed him up against the nearest wall, dropped to her knees and reached for his jeans. The door rocked shut and the interior plunged into darkness. The only light came from the overhead skylight.

Moonlight fell across her face as she stared up at him, but it wasn't enough. He wanted to see every expression, feel every reaction, hear every thought.

Groping to his left, he found the light switch. The overhead lights flicked on and a pale yellow glow pushed back the shadows and illuminated her face. Her cheeks flushed a bright pink and her lips trembled. Her eyes glittered with desire as she reached for him again. He didn't stop her this time. The air stalled in his lungs as he waited. And watched.

She slid the button free and worked the zipper down. His erection sprang hot and greedy toward her.

A drop of pearly liquid beaded on the ripe purple head and she reached out. She caught his essence and spread it in one sensual stroke of her fingertip from tip to root. A growl vibrated from deep in his chest and rumbled up his throat.

She wrapped her hand around him and he arched into her touch, his iron-hard sex dark and forbidden against her slender, pale fingers. She smiled up at him before she leaned forward. Her expression faded into one of serious intent as she lapped at him with her tongue, once, twice, before taking him into her mouth.

Her hair brushed against his belly. The soft, sweet-smelling strands teased his skin and stoked the fire that burned inside of him. Cole caught her long, silky hair and pulled the shimmering curtain away from her face. He watched as she sucked and licked and caused a pleasure so fierce he didn't think he could stand it.

He did.

He grew harder, hotter, heavier and she relished her effect on him. He saw it in the confident way she held him and the purposeful slide of her mouth up and down and... Damn, she felt good.

She took all of him, relished him, until he came so close to exploding.

"No!" He gasped and jerked back, catching himself just in time. He drew a shaky breath that did nothing to calm his thundering heart and everything to stir his hunger that much more. The scent of her— so potent and sweet and sexy—filled his nostrils, stirred his nerves and shook his already tenuous control. "Not like this." His cock throbbed, the feeling just this side of painful, and his balls ached, but he drew on what little control he had left. He grasped her shoulders and set her away from him.

She stared up, her eyes hot and luminous, mirroring the desperation he felt inside. But there was something else—the insecurity she tried so hard to hide with her racy comments and scandalous clothing.

Yeah, right, buddy. She might have been pretending, but that didn't mean that she felt anything for you other than the fear that you would run your mouth and ruin her bad reputation. Not then and sure as hell not now. She's out of here just as soon as she aces her finals and you call it quits with this farce of a marriage. And there isn't a damned thing you can do about it.

Like hell. He could change her mind if he wanted to. If.

But Cole had his own commitments. He was headed to the next rodeo, and the next. He lived out of a suitcase and he liked it that way. He sure as hell had no intention of settling down. Not in Lost Gun, and certainly not in Houston. The noise. The pollution. The clutter.

Hell, no.

He liked his space. His freedom. His spread outside of town suited him just fine. When he was home, that is, which wasn't very often.

No, he had a life to live, a career, and loving Nikki Barbie didn't figure into his plans.

He knew that, but it didn't stop him from picking her up and striding to the large bathroom. He wanted to touch every inch of her luscious little body in ways no man ever had or ever would.

Because Nikki Barbie was his.

At least for tonight.

He set her on her feet and turned on the water. Hot steam rose in the marble and glass enclosure. But the heat didn't come close to touching his rapidly soaring body temperature.

"I'm already wet," she told him with a smile. "You don't have to go to this much trouble."

"This isn't about trouble, darlin'. It's about erogenous zones." He grinned. "Since you aren't really all that experienced, I figured I'd give you a few lessons to get you back on the naughty list. Now," he said as he reached around for the straps of her sundress, "the female body has lots of hot spots."

"Such as?"

"Your neck for starters." He unfastened the halter-like top and let the straps fall away. The material fell to her waist, exposing her full breasts and rosy nipples. His gaze remained fixed on hers as he trailed his fingertips down either side of the smooth column of her neck, to where it curved into her shoulders.

She trembled. "What else?"

"Well, there are the obvious hot spots." He plucked the ripe tip of one nipple and drew a gasp from her passion-swollen lips before trailing a fingertip under the fullness of one breast, over the few inches of exposed skin until he reached the material bunched at her waist. He eased his fingers inside and pushed the dress over her hips until it slid down her legs. He stroked her bare mound with the pad of his thumb and watched her gaze darken.

"And then there are the not so obvious." He dropped to his knees and unfastened her shoes. His fingers lingered at the tender arch of one foot after he removed her shoes. "The feet are packed with nerve endings." He stroked the inside from her ankle to her toes before cupping her ankles with either hand and massaging gently.

"That does feel good."

"Just good?" He worked his way up her calves, the backs of her knees, her thighs, until he reached her sweet ass. He kneaded her, teasing the seam with his fingertips until she moaned.

"I've thought about touching you so many times

like this since the night of the wedding," he told her. "Too many times."

"I've thought about it, too."

He glanced up and caught her gaze. Her eyes were bright blue, fueled with desire and a dozen other emotions he couldn't name.

But he wanted to.

He wanted to know what she was thinking. Everything she was thinking.

"If you were dreaming this up right now, if this were your fantasy come to life, what would happen next? What would you want to happen next?"

She didn't even have to think. "You pick me up and carry me into the shower. We soap each other or we kiss. Or both."

He gave her a slow, lazy grin that made her blush despite her boldness. "I'll see what I can do." He stood, picked her up and stepped into the shower.

The door closed and the steam engulfed them. Hot water pelted his back and flowed over his skin. Easing her to her feet, he enjoyed the slow glide of her body down the slick, hard length of his.

"Turn around."

Nikki heard his deep voice, but she couldn't seem to comply. She'd pictured just this situation before and she was anxious to see if it lived up to her imagination.

Her gaze swept the length of him. His broad shoulders framed a wide chest sprinkled with crisp, dark hair that stretched from nipple to nipple in a V-shape. The brown silk narrowed and funneled down his abdomen and pelvis to disappear in the thatch of dark hair that surrounded his massive erection. His legs were braced apart, his thigh muscles taut, sprinkled with the same dark hair that covered his chest. His gaze was a bright, brilliant purple. His big, powerful form filled up the shower stall and blocked the spray of water. Water hammered the back of his head and ran in tiny rivulets over his shoulder, down his chest and abdomen to drip-drop off his swollen testicles.

She watched as he reached for the soap. He rubbed the bar between his large hands. Lather squeezed between his fingers and trailed down his powerful forearms.

"Turn around," he said again.

She obeyed this time and he stepped up behind her. She glanced down as his arms came around. His dark hands spread the white lather over her pale stomach. He cupped her breasts and slicked the soap over her nipples. She gasped.

He plucked and rolled the hard peaks until she trembled with sensation.

He paused then to reach for the soap. He didn't just lather his hands this time. Instead, he slid the bar down her quivering stomach, over the bare flesh of her sex.

"You're so soft and smooth," he murmured, his voice as thick as the erection pressing into the cleft of her buttocks.

He stroked her, rubbing the bar of soap in a sweet circular motion before moving down between her legs.

"Spread your legs for me." She widened her stance, giving him better access. The hard edge slid along the soft folds between her legs. The soap brushed her throbbing clitoris and intense pleasure rushed through her.

"Is this what happens in your fantasy?"

"No." He went still and her body hummed in expectancy. "It's better than any fantasy. Sweeter. Sharper. More intense." She felt his muscles ease. And then he moved, doing wickedly delicious things to her with the soap that told her he'd not only been waiting for her response, but he'd liked it.

He liked her.

He soaped her from head to toe, giving extra attention to every hot spot until Nikki shook with a need so fierce she couldn't stand it. She turned in his arms, desperate to feel him.

She touched everywhere she could reach, slicking her palms up and down his hard shoulder and hair-roughened chest. His taut hips and muscular buttocks. When she cupped his testicles, he growled.

He turned and flipped her water off. He grabbed

a towel from a nearby shelf and hooked it around her neck. Where the past few moments had been wild and fast, the brakes came on and everything slowed to a nice and easy and nerve-racking pace.

The fluffy white towel moved over her aroused body with an incredible slowness that made her want to scream. She didn't. Just when she thought she couldn't take any more, he pulled away. He wiped the moisture from his own body, scrubbed at his damp hair and then tossed the towel to the floor.

Before Nikki could draw breath, he reached for her. He pulled her flush against him. His hard length pressed into her stomach and he rubbed himself while his mouth devoured her in a deep, lusty kiss that made her insides clench and her nipples tingle.

Gripping her buttocks, he lifted her. She wrapped her legs around his waist and her arms around his neck. His hard, pulsing flesh grazed the sensitive area between her legs. The length rubbed against her slick folds as he turned and stepped from the shower stall.

He kept kissing her as he walked the few feet from the bathroom to the bedroom and eased her down on the king-size mattress.

Rounding the end of the bed, he grasped the shorts he'd shed. His shoulders bunched and his muscles flexed as he leaned down and retrieved a small foil packet from his pocket. He came to stand beside the bed, towering over her as he rolled the condom down his thick length with a swiftness that amazed her.

In that next instant, he was right where she wanted him, between her legs, his weight pressing her back into the mattress. His erection slid along her damp flesh, making her shudder and moan and arch toward him. He slid his hands beneath her, gripped her bottom and tilted her to take all of him. He plunged deep.

A shudder ripped through him and she touched him, trailing her hands over his hard buttocks, pulling him more securely inside. Her body clasped him, convulsing and quivering when he finally retreated. But he didn't leave her empty for long. He thrust into her again and again, building the pressure and pushing them both higher until, finally, he sent her soaring over the edge of ecstasy.

Nikki cried out Cole's name and dug her nails into his hard muscles as wave after wave of pure pleasure washed over her, drenching her senses for several heart-pounding moments.

She opened her eyes to find Cole poised above her, a fierce look on his face, his eyes gleaming with an intensity that reached inside of her and tugged at her heart.

When she gave him a blissful smile, he pounded into her one final time and let himself go. Every muscle in his body went rigid and his deep groan echoed in her ears.

He rolled over without breaking their intimate contact and cradled her on his chest, her head nestled in the curve of his shoulder. Large hands stroked up and down her back in a reverent motion that brought tears to Nikki's eyes.

But she didn't cry. There would be plenty of time for that later when everything was said and done. When Cole discovered the truth and turned his back on her once and for all.

For now, she held tight to the joy that rippled through her and focused on the man beneath her, the warmth of his neck against her cheek, the steady thud of his heart against her breast, the feel of his powerful arms locked around her.

It was all about this man and this moment.

This.

20

THE NEXT FEW hours passed much too quickly for Nikki. She and Cole had more exceptional sex and shared the most scrumptious peanut-butter-and-marshmallow sandwich in the wee hours of the morning, and then spent the rest of the morning talking. About everything from his brothers to her sisters, his excitement at the chance to go down in the history books with a record-breaking sixth saddle-bronc championship in a row and her nervousness at not knowing which sous-chef position to take. She'd heard back from two of the restaurants where she'd submitted resumes, and both had offered her a spot immediately after graduation.

All she had to do was prepare and cook a spectacular beef Wellington during her last and final class on the upcoming Friday—in just five days—and she would have her pick.

The Savoy.

That's what she told herself as she researched their website while Cole climbed into the shower. They'd checked for bank transactions to find that her mother had made a stop at a fast-food restaurant on the other side of Three Rivers and so they were pulling out and making the trek to the small town in search of more clues.

They wouldn't find any because Raylene was already on the road by now, heading for Port Aransas and the broken-down house that she intended to renovate into her dream bar.

Maybe.

That's what she told herself, desperate to ignore the truth—she knew where Raylene was going and she should just get it over with and tell Cole the truth.

She wanted to. At the same time, she knew that would kill the companionship they'd found over the past week and she just wasn't ready to do that. Not yet.

Another day, another step closer. Then she could be sure and break the news. She would.

She forced the thoughts aside and concentrated on The Savoy's menu blazing in full color on the computer screen in front of her. An endless list of the most upscale gourmet offerings imaginable. There was everything from marinated beef filet with port-wine reduction to rosemary-crusted lamb with mint-cream sauce. The appetizers were equally complicated. The desserts were light and balanced. And there wasn't a grilled cheese or a peanut-butter sandwich in sight.

The realization stirred a pang of sadness that must have shown on her face because Cole stalled in the hallway, a towel around his waist, water dripping from his still damp hair, and gave her a curious look.

"What's wrong?"

Everything.

"Nothing." She killed the web connection, closed the lid on the laptop and pushed to her feet. "I really should get dressed if we're going to pull out within the hour."

And then she walked away before she did something really stupid, like throw herself into his arms and admit that the feelings pushing and pulling at her went much deeper than lust.

Falling in love with Cole Chisholm was not part of her plan. While they did share a passion for a good grilled cheese sandwich, they were still all wrong for each other. He was Cole Chisholm, as beautiful and sexy and wild as the broncs he rode, and she was not-so-wild Nikki Barbie.

Despite the crazy, exceptional, extraordinary sex last night.

She couldn't fall in love with him.

SHE'D FALLEN IN LOVE with him.

Nikki finally admitted the truth to herself as she sat in a small diner on the outskirts of Three Rivers—across from the fast-food place where Raylene Barbie had swiped her credit card less than twenty-four hours before—and watched Cole cross the street to ask the usual questions.

Have you seen this woman?

Is she still in the area?

Do you know where she's going?

She hadn't wanted to love him. She'd feared loving him, because it would mean putting herself on the line and risking his rejection. As long as she believed that a man like him could never be serious about someone like her, there was no need to blurt out her feelings.

No risk. No rejection. No pain.

The thing was, the notion of never feeling his arms around her again, of never sitting next to him at a pickle festival, or sharing a snack late at night, or never again making wild, passionate love to him hurt her far worse than the notion of giving up her dream of being a chef.

She loved him, all right.

She'd always loved him, ever since he'd taken her hand that time and walked her home when she'd been in kindergarten.

She'd loved him every moment since, though she'd

done her damnedest to pass it off as a bad case of
lust, which hadn't been too difficult considering her
nonexistent sex life.

Cole Chisholm *was* sex, with his smoldering bedroom eyes, his teasing grin and seductive mouth. But
his appeal went even deeper than a great body or a
handsome face, or wicked hands, or the fact that he
knew how to use them.

He drew her to him. The gentle, tender boy he'd
been who'd huddled with his brothers in the back of
a rusted-out Chevy. The grown man he was now,
who volunteered his time to give advice to a bunch
of junior mutton busters and judge a pickle competition. The man who cherished his brothers enough to
drive clear across Texas to retrieve a bunch of cash
in the hope that it will help them make peace with
the past. The man who teased and smiled and made
her feel every bit a wild, wicked woman no matter
what she was wearing.

She loved him.

And he loved the idea of her.

Because he didn't really know the real woman.
Sure, he knew she wasn't all she was cracked up
to be in her bad-girl getup, but he didn't know that
she'd deceived him.

That she was still deceiving him.

"He was a liar and a cheat." She remembered his

words when he'd spoken of his father. The bitterness in his voice. The resentment.

He was sure to feel the same thing for her when he discovered she was no better than the man who'd betrayed him and his brothers for a huge wad of cash and a bottle of liquor.

And she wouldn't blame him because she was no better.

But she wanted to be.

She wanted to be someone he could depend on. Trust. *Love*.

And suddenly nothing else mattered but that she tell him the truth right here and now. Regardless of the consequences.

Because of them.

Because the last thing she needed was to spend another day talking to him, laughing with him, loving him.

It was time to come clean. For his sake, and her own.

"They remember her." His deep voice slid into her ears and she glanced up just as he slid into the seat across from her. "Not that it matters. She didn't mention where she was going, or drop a hint what her next move might be. Looks like we're stuck here until she makes another move."

"No, we're not." She steeled herself and gathered every ounce of strength she had deep down inside.

Her gaze met his. "We don't have to stay here. We can pull out today."

"What are you talking about?"

She tamped down a wave of fear and held tight to her newfound courage. "I know where she's going."

21

HE HADN'T SAID a word in the past hour and a half.

Not since they'd left Three Rivers and she'd explained her last conversation with her mother and the all-important fact that she'd had a hunch about the woman's destination all along.

No *Why didn't you tell me sooner?*

Or *How could you do such a thing?*

No ranting and raving and telling her what a liar she was and how much he hated her. Nothing but cold, thick, unforgiving silence.

Because he doesn't feel anything for you. You betrayed him and now you're not deserving of any of his feelings. No hatred. No love. Nada.

He was simply ambivalent.

Thankfully.

She didn't have to worry about a huge fight along the way, or a tear-filled goodbye when they parted ways. They would reach Port Aransas, locate her mother, recover the money and go their separate ways, no emotion involved.

Talk about easy.

But there was nothing easy about the confrontation that followed when they finally reached the run-down house on a small stretch of deserted beach near the far end of Mustang Island, just minutes down the road from the coastal hot spot of Port Aransas, Texas. A faint breeze blew in off the water, stirring a chill in the cool October air. The waves rolled and crashed, mimicking the flood of emotion roiling inside Nikki.

"What are you doing here?" Raylene Barbie demanded when they rounded the house and walked up onto the back deck where she sat. The house stood empty and dark behind her, the paint peeled away, the windows busted out. Raylene pushed to her feet, her expression filled with surprise rather than guilt, and Nikki had her first hint that something wasn't quite right.

Something besides Nikki's strained relationship with the man standing beside her.

"Just hand it over and we'll be on our way," Cole said, his gaze darting past Raylene to the open doorway and the sparse furnishings inside. As if he could spot the one thing that had lured him clear across the state.

"Don't come here and bark orders at me," Raylene started, but Cole wasn't about to let her finish.

"Hand it over or I'll go in and take it."

Fighting words, Nikki knew, but Raylene was too busy being confused to rise to the challenge. "Hand what over?"

"The money," Nikki chimed in, eager to diffuse the volatile situation before it ignited. "We know you took it, Mom. Just give it back—all of it—and we'll be on our way."

"I don't know what you're talking about." Raylene sank back down to her worn lounge chair, her shoulders slumped as if the air had rushed out of her at the mention of the cash. "I don't have any money, nor do I know anything about any money. If I did, I wouldn't be drowning my sorrows in this cheap-ass can of beer." She motioned to the inexpensive brand sitting on the table in front of her. "I would have picked up some of the imported stuff. Maybe even a lime or two. And I'd be on the phone right now trying to do something about all of this." She motioned around her. "It used to be so much prettier." She seemed almost sad and Nikki's chest tightened.

She'd never seen her mother so pensive and…regretful, even. As if nothing were going according to plan.

She knew the feeling.

"Mom, it's okay. We just need the money back."

"I don't know what you're talking about."

"Listen, lady," Cole started, his patience obviously shot, "I'm through wasting time. Hand it over right now."

Most women would have cowered beneath Cole's stare, but Raylene wasn't most women. She'd held her own for too many years to let anyone intimidate her. "I didn't invite either of you here. Go back to Lost Gun, back to matrimonial bliss and all that crap, and leave me alone." She rubbed a hand over her suddenly weary face. "I've got a lot to figure out."

Cole arched an eyebrow. "Like how to spend my money?"

"Actually, I'm using more brain power on how I'm going to get by without any money of my own," she snapped. Her gaze swiveled to Nikki. "Get him out of here before I call the cops. This is private property and I don't want you here. Either of you." For all her bravado, her hands trembled ever so slightly.

"Go ahead." Two fingers dove into his pocket and he handed over his cell. The phone hit the wooden table with a dull *clunk*. "Call them and tell them you have a trespasser. And then I'll tell them I've got a thief in possession of a hundred thousand dollars in stolen bank bills."

"I don't know what you're talking about."

"The duffel bag, Mom," Nikki chimed in again. "The one that was sitting in my living room. We know you took it. I saw you pick up something when you left. I thought it was your purse, but then Cole found his bag missing and, well, I knew. You took it."

"That old thing? Well, yeah, sure, I took it. But I didn't steal any money. I wouldn't do that. No matter how hard the times." She shrugged. "Hell, I didn't even know there was any money in it. I just thought it belonged to this one." She motioned to Cole. "I took it just to piss him off."

"So you didn't open it?"

"Hell, no. I just tossed it in the Dumpster out back." She snorted. "Just to teach him a lesson for what he did."

"You threw it in the Dumpster? The one in back of the bar?"

"Damn straight, I did."

"Like hell," Cole thundered. "What do you take me for? An idiot?"

Raylene shrugged. "Hey, if the boot fits—"

"Mom," Nikki cut in. "This is serious. We've come a long way. You have to tell us the truth."

"That's what I'm doing." And while Raylene had never been the most sympathetic and understanding mother, she'd always told the truth. A straight-shooter, she called herself, and Nikki couldn't help but believe her.

"She tossed it," Nikki heard herself say.

"And you didn't open it?" Cole pressed Raylene. "Not even a peek?"

"Trust me, if I had I wouldn't have thrown it in the Dumpster. And I sure as hell wouldn't be sitting here in this hell hole right now, not with a plush Holiday Inn just down the road."

"When does the Dumpster get picked up?" Cole asked Nikki and she knew that he'd finally bought Raylene's explanation.

"Every Friday when it's full. If not, they leave it until the following week."

"Today is Sunday. That means…" He let loose a series of curse words that burned even Nikki's ears, and she'd grown up with Raylene who could give any sailor a run for his money. "They already picked it up."

"Maybe," Nikki said, desperate to say something to ease the sudden tightness in his muscles. "If it wasn't full, they might have left it. There's still a chance." While it had taken them six days to track Raylene across Texas because they'd been following a slow transaction trail, they were technically only twelve hours away from Lost Gun. If they left right now—

"We have to go," Cole cut in, obviously following her train of thought. "Now." And then he turned and headed for the RV parked in the driveway.

"Was there really one hundred thousand dollars

stashed in that duffel bag?" Raylene's voice followed Nikki.

"Yes."

"If that don't beat it all…"

THE DUMPSTER WAS EMPTY.

They discovered that hard truth in the wee hours of the morning when they finally rolled into Lost Gun and headed straight for the Giddyup.

A single bulb gleamed overhead, casting a pale glow on the back parking area and the large green metal container that sat just off to the side of the back door. There were a few bags of trash inside, but it was obvious that the Dumpster had been emptied not very long ago, the contents hauled out to a huge landfill that sat a few miles outside the city limits.

It was the county dump spot and overflowing with mounds and mounds of trash from every Dumpster within a sixty-mile radius. Which meant that Cole and his brothers would have another four months of digging before they found the bag.

If they found it.

"So what happens now?" Nikki asked a stoic-faced Cole.

"I break the news to Jesse and we figure out what to do next. I'm more than happy to pay it back myself, but the whole point was to give back the actual money."

So that everyone in town would know that they'd been telling the truth all these years, and while Cole claimed that he didn't care, she could see that he did.

He cared, all right.

He cared a lot.

"I need to get out of here."

"I'm sorry," she blurted when he turned away. "I really am. I should have told you. I just didn't know for sure at first and I didn't want to say anything when it was just a theory. And then when I knew, I couldn't say anything. Not without you thinking what you're thinking right now."

"Which is?"

"What a horrible person I am."

He actually looked surprised. "That's not what I'm thinking."

"It's not?" She swallowed the lump sitting in her throat and focused on the thread of hope coursing through her. A crazy, delusional feeling because it wouldn't change anything. She knew that, yet she couldn't help but ask anyway. "Then what are you thinking?"

"That you should have trusted me enough to tell me the truth."

"Why?"

Because I love you and you love me.

That's what she wanted him to say.

But as much as she wanted him to say the words,

she feared them, as well. Because as much as she'd tried to convince herself otherwise, she was still Raylene Barbie's daughter.

A truth that had nothing to do with the risqué clothes that she wore or the way she flirted her ass off when the situation called for it, and everything to do with the man standing in front of her.

The only man she'd ever really and truly wanted.

She'd been so fearful of being stuck in Lost Gun, of following in her mother's footsteps despite her best efforts when truthfully, she was doing just that by running off to Houston to pursue her culinary dream.

She was doing just what Raylene had done her entire life—she was running from commitment. From love.

She'd never let any man get close to her because she'd feared being caught. Stuck.

A chip off the old block.

Like hell.

She wasn't running from commitment because there was nothing on the table. No declaration of love. Not even a half-hearted *I really like you.*

And so she wasn't running from anything. She was following her dreams, just as Cole was about to follow his straight to Vegas, to buckle number six and a win that would put him in the record book and turn him from a rodeo star to a bona fide legend.

He had his dreams, and she had hers, and they should just call it quits.

She knew that, but she pressed anyway because she couldn't stifle the hope that he would prove her wrong. "Why should I trust you? Because we're 'married'?" She shook her head, determined to ignore the feelings pushing and pulling inside of her. She wasn't taking a chance and putting herself out there unless she knew for certain that he felt the same way. Unless he said the words. "It's not real," she rushed on. "I'm not your wife and you're not my husband. We're not even friends."

Say something.

Tell me I'm wrong.

Delusional.

Crazy.

"You're right," he said after a tense, silent moment, killing any hope that she had that things could actually work between them. "We're not friends."

"Exactly." She blinked back the hotness prickling behind her eyes. "I don't even like you."

He gave her a dark look. "And I sure as hell don't like you."

"And my mom's gone now, so I don't need you to help me keep her away."

"And the money's gone, so I don't need to stick around here and ward off a bunch of marriage-minded women."

"So it's over," she murmured, forcing the words past the sudden lump in her throat.

"Over." It seemed as if he said the word more to convince himself than her.

"Good luck in Vegas," she murmured. "I know you'll do great." And then she fought down the crazy urge to throw herself into his arms and hold on for dear life, and walked away.

HE WASN'T GOING after her.

Cole steeled himself against the near-overwhelming urge and watched as she topped the stairs and disappeared inside the apartment.

The door shut and the lights flicked on inside and still, he didn't move.

It's over, buddy. She said so. You said so. Get over it and get moving.

He wanted to.

He wanted to turn and walk away the way he would have with any other woman.

That's all she was.

Even as he tried to convince himself of that, he knew deep down inside that it was just a bunch of B.S.

Nikki was different. Special.

A liar.

He reminded himself of that all-important fact, but damned if he actually believed it. She might have withheld information, but she hadn't done it because she was untrustworthy or unreliable. And certainly not because it had been second nature to her.

She'd simply wanted to protect her mother.

She loved Raylene in spite of everything.

Just as he loved his father.

The truth rumbled from down deep, stirring a rush of denial as fierce as the emotion himself. Because Silas didn't deserve his love. Not then, and certainly not now.

Not ever.

Maybe not, but as Nikki had said, this wasn't about Silas. It was about Cole. About what he felt deep inside.

What he'd tried to deny for so long because he hadn't wanted to feel anything where the man was concerned.

He hadn't wanted to feel anything now. Because it made things easier. Safer. He could come and go as he pleased and not worry about hurting anyone, or being hurt the way he'd been so many times in the past.

Most of all, he didn't have to worry about loving someone who didn't love him back.

Like now.

He fought the truth and turned on his heel. He didn't love her and she didn't love him, and that was good.

Great.

He held tight to the thought, climbed into the RV, steered the monstrous beast back onto the road, and headed toward Jesse's place. After a quick stop to explain the situation to his brother, he'd be on his way to Vegas.

Finally.

If only he could shake the feeling that he was about to make the biggest mistake of his life.

22

NIKKI SPENT THE night tossing and turning and replaying her last conversation with Cole, and wishing with all of her heart that it had gone differently.

Because she did love him.

She'd finally admitted as much to herself early that morning as she'd stared at the ceiling and tried to forget the way it had felt to fall asleep in his arms and the overwhelming knowledge that she would never, *ever* feel that way again.

No falling asleep in his arms. No waking up to him the next morning. No laughing over a midnight snack or stargazing from the top of his RV.

The thoughts haunted her as she made her way downstairs early the next morning and rounded the building toward the bar's front entrance. She'd left the place in Colby's hands over the past week while she'd trekked across the state, but she was back now.

At least for the next few days until she took her finals.

Just because she loved him, she wasn't abandoning her plans to stay home in Lost Gun and waste away at the Giddyup while Cole went on about his business. She had to keep going, to move forward.

To stop looking back.

All the more reason to get inside and get to work.

She unlocked the door and headed through the dim interior. The place was quiet. Peaceful. Perfect for an entire day spent working in the kitchen. Uninterrupted. Focused.

Talk about nirvana.

Even so, she couldn't manage to summon the usual excitement when she walked into the kitchen. No, all she could think about was Cole and how he'd stood downstairs long after she'd gone into her apartment.

As if he'd been waiting for her to change her mind.

As if he'd wanted her to.

As if.

He could have said something if he'd felt differently, but he hadn't. He'd let her walk away, run away, and he hadn't said a word to the contrary.

Which was fine. Really. She didn't need Cole Chisholm anyway. She had her entire future stretched out in front of her. A new apartment waiting in Houston courtesy of the money she'd saved over the past few years. An internship at the infamous Savoy because she was surely going to ace her finals.

If she didn't drop dead of a heart attack first.

She clutched her chest and stared at the young man who'd just walked into the kitchen.

"Colby?" She eyed the thick gold chain that he wore with what looked like a brand-new shirt and stiff, starched denim. "What are you doing here so early?"

"I saw your light on last night when I was on my way home from Bingo, so I knew you were back. I wanted to show you my new look." He indicated the new belt clinging to his slim waist. "Pretty cool, huh?"

"It's nice."

"It's more than nice. When April gets back, she'll realize what a mistake she made by marrying that guy and she'll give me a chance. I'll take her to a fancy restaurant in Austin and buy her something expensive and she'll see that I can give her even more than that rodeo star she married. She'll divorce him and we'll live happily ever after."

"Colby, I know you really like April, but that's not going to happen. It doesn't matter how much money you have…" Her words trailed off before she even finished her sentence as several all-important things registered. *New look. Fancy restaurant. Something expensive.*

Which wouldn't have been a big deal, except this was Colby who made minimum wage. He couldn't afford any of the above. Unless...

"You found the duffel bag, didn't you?"

Guilt washed over his expression and she knew even before he said, "If you mean a black duffel bag with a red zipper, no." He shook his head profusely. "I didn't find it."

"Yes, you did. You just described it."

"That was just a lucky guess."

"And the money for the new clothes?"

"I saved it up." She gave him an unflinching stare and he buckled in a few seconds. "Okay, I found it." He shrugged. "I know I shouldn't have taken it, but I thought maybe God was trying to make up for the fact that he let April marry that Jimmy Barber. I thought this was my chance to impress her and maybe get her back."

Because he loved her and he was more than willing to lay it all on the line to show her.

Even though he knew the odds were against him and April might not love him back.

He didn't care. He was going to give it a shot anyway. Consequences be damned.

Her heartbeat kicked into high gear and she knew in a startling instant that she wasn't just going to sit by and do nothing.

"Where's the rest of the money?" she asked Colby.

"You're going to make me give it back, aren't you?"

"You can keep the clothes, but yes, you've got to give the rest of it back." When he didn't look convinced, she added, "It's the right thing to do." Even more, it was going to give her one more chance to see Cole Chisholm and tell him that she loved him and wanted to spend the rest of her life with him.

She did.

And if he doesn't feel the same way?

She was going to tell him anyway.

If he hadn't already left, that is.

"Get the money," she told Colby, "and meet me in the parking lot." And then she headed for the door.

HE WAS LEAVING.

That's what Cole told himself as he headed out to the training facility to meet with his new driver. Eli had dropped the bomb just last night that he wouldn't be heading out to Vegas with him. After Cole had dropped the bomb about the money to Jesse last night.

"I'm sorry, bud," he told his brother, but he needn't have said the words. Jesse hadn't blamed him for anything. They'd tried to do the right thing and they'd almost succeeded.

Almost.

Not that it would have changed anything anyhow.

That's what Cole told himself, he just wasn't so sure he believed it anymore. Because he'd changed.

He didn't feel so indifferent inside. So contained. So suppressed.

He felt, period. And that was good. Useless, but good.

It had helped him offer up a genuine congratulations when Eli had called to tell Cole that he'd asked his sweetie to marry him and she'd said yes.

"I hate to bail on you, son, but you'll have to find another driver. 'Sides, I'm too old anyhow. I'm liable to wrap that big ole bus around a telephone pole or something. You need to find someone young to take my place. Someone who can stick with you for a while."

Married?

Eli?

The man had been single for as long as Cole could remember. Sure, he'd gotten up close and comfortable with the ladies over the years, but he'd never gotten serious with one.

Until he'd met the right one.

Cole shook away the thought, pulled into the parking lot and walked into the office area to meet the new guy that Jesse had found for him at the last minute. That very morning to be exact.

At least that's what Jesse had said when he'd left a voice mail a half hour ago.

"I found the right person for you."

But there was no one waiting in the small office area. Just an empty duffel bag.

The duffel bag.

He grabbed the familiar black canvas and yanked open the red zipper. Sure enough, it was his. The same bag he'd used to stash the money.

"Colby found it the day after we left when he was taking out the trash and pulled it out of the Dumpster." The soft voice sounded directly behind him and he turned to see Nikki standing in the doorway.

She wore a Giddyup T-shirt tucked into a fitted black miniskirt that hugged her in all the right places. But it wasn't the outfit that stalled the air in his lungs. It was the gleam in her eyes.

"I don't understand," he managed, despite a suddenly dry throat.

"Colby found the money, and spent exactly one hundred and forty-seven dollars. He was going to spend more, but luckily he's conscientious. He didn't have time to go car shopping because he was filling in for me at the bar. Otherwise, you would have been missing a lot more."

"But there's nothing here."

"I stopped by Jesse's when I was looking for you this morning. I told him about the money, handed it over and he sent me out here. He said you needed a driver." A grin tugged at the corner of her mouth. "I'd like to apply for the job."

"I don't understand."

"I'm trying to tell you that I love you. That I've always loved you. And that I'm willing to follow you to the ends of the Earth or, in this case, Vegas."

"What about Houston?"

"Who needs a new apartment and a fancy internship?" She shrugged. "I'm giving my stash to my mom. She can use it to fix up the old house and finally have her dream bar right on the beach."

"What about your finals?"

"Oh, I intend to take those. I want my degree, even if I don't think it'll come in very handy out at the bar."

"You're going to stay on?"

"I'm going to turn it into an old-fashioned diner where the locals can get a good grilled cheese sandwich and a decadent piece of Dr. Pepper cake. I was hoping you might help me out, maybe wait a few tables. After Vegas, that is."

"I can't do that."

"Because you don't love me," she stated. "That's it, isn't it? I convinced myself on the drive over here that you didn't say the words because maybe, just maybe you were as scared as I was, but that's not it, is it? You don't feel the same."

Doubt rushed through him, followed by a sense

of joy so profound that he knew he could never turn and walk away from her. Not now. Not twenty years from now. Not never.

What's more, he didn't want to walk away. To run. To keep running the way he'd been doing for so many years.

It was time to stop. To love someone. To trust someone enough to let them love him.

A strange sense of peace stole through him, and for the first time he didn't feel the itch to get going.

There was no more chasing his freedom.

Because he'd already found it.

Real freedom was loving and being loved, and it was right here, right now, right at his fingertips.

It was Nikki.

"I do love you." He said the words he'd felt for so long but refused to admit. "More than anything."

Her panic faded into a look of pure delight. "Does that mean I get the job?"

"'Til death do us part."

"That sounds like a proposal more than job offer."

His grin faded as he stared deep into her eyes. "Will you marry me, Nikki, and make me the happiest man alive?"

"I will," she murmured. "I do." And then she kissed him and left no doubt in his mind that she meant it.

Epilogue

IT WAS THE biggest wedding the small town of Lost Gun, Texas, had ever seen.

Nikki Barbie stood at the door of a makeshift tent and peeked past the drapes at the scene spread before her. Banquet tables draped in crisp white linen filled the massive tents that had been set up on an empty stretch of land just twenty miles outside of town. The property was located just a few miles down the road from Pete Gunner's massive spread, overlooking a winding creek and a massive waterfall. A crescent moon hung in the clear sky, surrounded by twinkling stars. Candles floated in giant crystal bowls at the center of each table, giving the entire place a surreal-like quality that made for a picturesque backdrop as all three of the infamous Chisholm brothers tied the knot in a triple ceremony that had taken Nikki and the other two brides over six months to plan.

A spring ceremony with lots of flowers and a crispness in the evening air.

There was a tent set up to house the food and

a giant array of homemade desserts that had been trucked in from the Giddyup diner, formerly the town's most notorious honky-tonk.

It now served up the best homemade dishes for a fifty-mile radius and had been an obvious choice for the massive event.

It was Nikki's wedding, after all, and she'd wanted all of her grammy Ruth's favorites in attendance. Luckily Gracie and Sabrina had fallen in love with the entire menu and had been more than eager to have Nikki provide the food.

Not personally, of course. She'd had way too much to do to pull that off. Rather, she'd handed over her recipe box to a group of well-trained cooks who'd done the recipes proud. The delicious smells floating through the air proved as much and reminded her of Grammy Ruth.

Which explained why Raylene Barbie sat on the front row of the ceremony area, looking as if she wanted to throw up.

While Nikki had stopped burying the past, Raylene was still in full denial. But at least she was here to see her youngest daughter tie the knot for the second time—or so she and everyone in town thought.

Nikki and Cole had never told anyone that the first time had been a fake. She glanced down at the monstrous ring he'd given her during their road trip. A fake, or so she'd thought. But the ring, like the relationship, had turned out to be the real deal, and so they'd spent the past months living happily ever after.

But it was time to make it official. Particularly since Nikki had a special wedding present for Cole.

She touched her still-flat stomach and gave in to a small smile. A present for them both.

Her gaze went to her mother. While she looked as hard and unyielding as ever, Raylene had actually softened some since Nikki had handed over her nest egg to fund Raylene's dream. She'd been so stunned that she'd actually stopped pushing her daughters so hard and started to focus on her own life.

Her own love.

Nikki eyed the man who sat next to her. Her bartender, or so she'd told everyone when she'd arrived from Port Aransas with the man in tow. But there was just something about the way he slid his arm around her and she leaned into him just so that said he was much more than the typical one-night stand.

That, and he'd been her "bartender" for three months now. She'd mentioned him in every phone conversation, and not the usual *"He's a great kisser."*

She'd talked about him, his three children from a previous marriage, his grandkids, the fact that he'd retired from the army to spend his days relaxing on the Texas coast. Things that Raylene had never cared about before.

Until now.

Until him.

Nikki smiled and let the drapes slide to before she turned her attention to the two other brides standing in wait beside her.

"It's a packed house," Gracie remarked. She was Jesse's soon-to-be bride and once upon a time, the mayor of Lost Gun. She adjusted her gloves and smiled. "We probably should have tried to whittle down the list a little more."

Instead of inviting practically *everyone*.

But they hadn't wanted to leave anyone out and so they'd had the genius idea to open up the celebration to any and all.

The Chisholm brothers had agreed.

Which had caught Nikki by surprise.

While she knew that Cole had made his peace with the past and didn't hold a grudge against the townsfolk who'd been less than supportive over the years, she hadn't been too sure about Jesse and Billy.

But they, too, had been agreeable to an obscene amount of invites and a ridiculous wedding budget.

Because they'd made peace with the past.

The money—with the exception of one hundred and forty-seven dollars, which they'd simply failed to uncover out at Big Earl's place—had been given back to the bank from which it had been stolen, along with a healthy endowment check to several local charities on the bank's behalf. Not that the money had changed anyone's opinions.

People thought what they wanted to think, despite the truth.

No, giving the money back hadn't changed any opinions. Rather, it had changed the Chisholm brothers themselves. They'd done the right thing, and while it could never make up for the wrong that their father had done, they'd at least proven something to themselves and closed the book on that chapter of their lives. The money had been found and returned, and that was that.

Jesse slept better at night.

And Billy was even more friendly than usual.

And Cole…Cole had stopped running and started living.

He'd won his sixth buckle and set a new record for consecutive championships, and now he was ready to trade in his career for a beautiful stretch of land where he intended to breed the best cutting horses in the nation.

This stretch of land.

Once the vows had been recited and the cake cut, that is.

"It's time," Sabrina said, glancing at her watch. She was Billy's intended and a country girl at heart despite her addiction to designer couture. She reached for the bouquet waiting in a vase nearby. "Ladies." She gave Gracie and Nikki a huge smile and a wink. "Let's get hitched."

* * * * *

COMING NEXT MONTH FROM

Available March 18, 2014

#791 A SEAL'S KISS
Uniformly Hot!
by Tawny Weber

What do you get when you bring together a hot navy SEAL—aka
Aiden Masters—who's addicted to rules, and a sexy free spirit like
Sage Taylor, who sets out to break every rule she can? Sparks!

#792 NOTHING TO HIDE
The Wrong Bed
by Isabel Sharpe

How much skimpy lingerie does it take to seduce a billionaire?
Clothing designer Allie McDonald isn't sure, but her lakeside
catch-and-release plan backfires when sexy Jonas Meyer hooks
her instead!

#793 BREAKAWAY
Last Bachelor Standing
by Nancy Warren

Max Varo isn't about to invest in a small struggling Alaskan airline.
But the heart—and body!—of this committed bachelor says
otherwise when he meets sexy bush pilot Claire Lundstrom.

#794 THE MIGHTY QUINNS: MALCOLM
The Mighty Quinns
by Kate Hoffmann

As an adventure-travel guide in New Zealand, Malcolm Quinn lives
for a challenge. His latest: seducing writer Amy Engalls. Amy is
like climbing without a harness—exhilarating, heart-pumping...and
dangerous. Because there's nothing to catch him if he falls.

**YOU CAN FIND MORE INFORMATION ON UPCOMING HARLEQUIN® TITLES,
FREE EXCERPTS AND MORE AT WWW.HARLEQUIN.COM.**

HBCNM0314

REQUEST YOUR FREE BOOKS!
2 FREE NOVELS PLUS 2 FREE GIFTS!

HARLEQUIN *Blaze*

red-hot reads!

YES! Please send me 2 FREE Harlequin® Blaze™ novels and my 2 FREE gifts (gifts are worth about $10). After receiving them, if I don't wish to receive any more books, I can return the shipping statement marked "cancel." If I don't cancel, I will receive 4 brand-new novels every month and be billed just $4.74 per book in the U.S. or $4.96 per book in Canada. That's a savings of at least 14% off the cover price. It's quite a bargain. Shipping and handling is just 50¢ per book in the U.S. and 75¢ per book in Canada.* I understand that accepting the 2 free books and gifts places me under no obligation to buy anything. I can always return a shipment and cancel at any time. Even if I never buy another book, the two free books and gifts are mine to keep forever.

150/350 HDN F4WC

Name	(PLEASE PRINT)	
Address		Apt. #
City	State/Prov.	Zip/Postal Code

Signature (if under 18, a parent or guardian must sign)

Mail to the **Harlequin® Reader Service:**
IN U.S.A.: P.O. Box 1867, Buffalo, NY 14240-1867
IN CANADA: P.O. Box 609, Fort Erie, Ontario L2A 5X3

Want to try two free books from another line?
Call 1-800-873-8635 or visit www.ReaderService.com.

* Terms and prices subject to change without notice. Prices do not include applicable taxes. Sales tax applicable in N.Y. Canadian residents will be charged applicable taxes. Offer not valid in Quebec. This offer is limited to one order per household. Not valid for current subscribers to Harlequin Blaze books. All orders subject to credit approval. Credit or debit balances in a customer's account(s) may be offset by any other outstanding balance owed by or to the customer. Please allow 4 to 6 weeks for delivery. Offer available while quantities last.

Your Privacy—The Harlequin® Reader Service is committed to protecting your privacy. Our Privacy Policy is available online at www.ReaderService.com or upon request from the Harlequin Reader Service.

We make a portion of our mailing list available to reputable third parties that offer products we believe may interest you. If you prefer that we not exchange your name with third parties, or if you wish to clarify or modify your communication preferences, please visit us at www.ReaderService.com/consumerschoice or write to us at Harlequin Reader Service Preference Service, P.O. Box 9062, Buffalo, NY 14269. Include your complete name and address.

HB13R2

SPECIAL EXCERPT FROM

HARLEQUIN

Blaze

Kate Hoffmann starts a new chapter in her
beloved miniseries with the New Zealand
Quinns—Rogan, Ryan and the namesake of the
April 2014 release

The Mighty Quinns: Malcolm

Mal is the protector of his family, and right now
they need protection from nosy reporters.
Like Amy Engalls. She wants a story...unless he
can give her something better....

Amy could barely catch her breath. It was as if she was tumbling
down a mountainside and she couldn't gain a foothold. But
now that she'd gained momentum, she didn't want to stop.

Mal was the kind of guy she could only dream about
having—handsome, charming, fearless. And now, she'd been
handed the chance to be with him, to experience something
she might never find in her life again. Sure, she'd had lovers in
the past, but they'd never made her feel wild and uninhibited.
Just once, she wanted to be with a man who could make her
heart pound and her body ache.

Just a week ago, she'd been curled up on her sofa in her
Brooklyn flat, eating a pint of cherry chocolate-chip ice cream

HBEXP79798

and watching romantic comedies. That had been her life, waiting for Mr. Right. Well, it was time to stop waiting. She'd found Mr. Right Now here on the beach in New Zealand.

This wouldn't be about love or even affection. It would be about pure, unadulterated passion. This would be the adventure she'd never been brave enough to take. She wasn't about to pass this opportunity by. If she couldn't leave New Zealand with a story, then she'd leave with a damn good memory.

At the bedroom door, Mal stopped. He grabbed her hands and pinned them above her head, searching her gaze. "Are you sure this is what you want?" he murmured, pressing his hips against hers.

The quilt fell away, leaving Amy dressed only in her underwear. She could feel his desire beneath the faded fabric of his jeans—he was already completely aroused. Amy wanted to touch him there, to smooth her fingers over the hard ridge of his erection. She could be bold, too. "Yes," she said, pushing back with her body.

He kissed her again, his lips and tongue demanding a response. She did her best to match his intensity, and when he groaned, Amy knew that *she* was exactly what he wanted.

Pick up THE MIGHTY QUINNS: MALCOLM
by Kate Hoffmann, available March 18
wherever you buy Harlequin® Blaze® books.

When opposites attract, sparks fly!

What do you get when you bring together a hot navy SEAL—aka Aiden Masters—who's addicted to rules, and a sexy free spirit like Sage Taylor, who sets out to break every rule she can? Sparks!

Don't miss the next chapter of the Uniformly Hot! miniseries

A SEAL's Kiss

by *USA TODAY* bestselling author
Tawny Weber!

Available March 18, 2014,
wherever you buy Harlequin Blaze books.

HARLEQUIN®

***Blaze*®**

Red-Hot Reads
www.Harlequin.com

HB79795